"If you'd let me bed down in your barn tonight, I'd be much obliged...

"But I want to repay you. Maybe I can stick around for a few days, help you out."

"I appreciate the offer," Leah replied, "but I don't really think you're going to feel like cleaning stalls tomorrow. Isn't there somewhere you need to be?" she asked, though the idea of another pair of hands pitching in was sorely tempting.

"I'm in no hurry."

Leah searched his face, desperately wanting to go along with what he'd suggested.

"You wouldn't have to pay me wages or anything, just room and board. How about it?" He stuck out his hand.

"Let's see how you feel in the morning," Leah replied, cautiously putting her hand in his. Immediately his fingers tightened. Warm, strong and reassuring. His gaze remained steady, as though he had nothing to hide.

As he released her hand, his face relaxed into a mesmerizing grin.

"Fair enough," she said without realizing it. What had she just g

Dear Reader,

Special Edition is pleased to bring you six exciting love stories to help you celebrate spring...and blossoming love.

To start off the month, don't miss *A Father for Her Baby* by Celeste Hamilton—a THAT'S MY BABY! title that features a pregnant amnesiac who is reunited with her long-ago fiancé. Now she must uncover the past in order to have a future with this irresistible hero and her new baby.

April offers Western romances aplenty! In the third installment of her action-packed HEARTS OF WYOMING series, Myrna Temte delivers *Wrangler.* A reticent lady wrangler has a mighty big secret, but sparks fly between her and the sexy lawman she's been trying very hard to avoid; the fourth book in the series will be available in July. Next, Pamela Toth brings us another heartwarming story in her popular BUCKLES & BRONCOS miniseries. In *Buchanan's Pride,* a feisty cowgirl rescues a stranded stranger—only to discover he's the last man on earth she should let into her heart!

There's more love on the range coming your way. *Finally His Bride* by Christine Flynn—part of THE WHITAKER BRIDES series—is an emotional reunion romance between two former sweethearts. Also the MEN OF THE DOUBLE-C RANCH series continues when a brooding Clay brother claims the woman he's never stopped wanting in *A Wedding For Maggie* by Allison Leigh. Finally, debut author Carol Finch shares an engaging story about a fun-loving rodeo cowboy who woos a romance-resistant single mom in *Not Just Another Cowboy.*

I hope you enjoy these stirring tales of passion, and each and every romance to come!

Sincerely,

Karen Taylor Richman
Senior Editor

Please address questions and book requests to:
Silhouette Reader Service
U.S.: 3010 Walden Ave., P.O. Box 1325, Buffalo, NY 14269
Canadian: P.O. Box 609, Fort Erie, Ont. L2A 5X3

PAMELA TOTH
BUCHANAN'S PRIDE

Published by Silhouette Books

America's Publisher of Contemporary Romance

To my daughter Melody Toth,
who has more talents than a diamond has facets,
and who is infinitely more precious.

And to my husband, Frank.
My forever starts with you.

 SILHOUETTE BOOKS

ISBN 0-373-24239-5

BUCHANAN'S PRIDE

Copyright © 1999 by Pamela Toth

Printed in U.S.A.

Books by Pamela Toth

Silhouette Special Edition

Thunderstruck #411
Dark Angel #515
Old Enough To Know Better #624
Two Sets of Footprints #729
A Warming Trend #760
Walk Away, Joe #850
The Wedding Knot #905
Rocky Mountain Rancher #951
*Buchanan's Bride #1012
*Buchanan's Baby #1017
*Buchanan's Return #1096
The Paternity Test #1138
†The Mail-Order Mix-Up #1197
*Buchanan's Pride #1239

Silhouette Romance

Kissing Games #500
The Ladybug Lady #595

*Buckles & Broncos
†The Winchester Brides

PAMELA TOTH

was born in Wisconsin, but grew up in Seattle, where she attended the University of Washington and majored in art. She still lives near Seattle with her two daughters and several Siamese cats. When she isn't writing, she enjoys reading, traveling, quilting and researching new story ideas.

The heroes of her books have won several *Romantic Times* WISH Awards and she has been nominated for five *Romantic Times* Reviewer's Choice Awards, including Best Series Romance for *Walk Away, Joe*. *Buchanan's Baby* and *Buchanan's Return* were on the *USA Today* bestseller list.

She loves hearing from readers and can be reached at P.O. Box 5845, Bellevue, WA 98006. For a personal reply, a stamped, self-addressed envelope is appreciated.

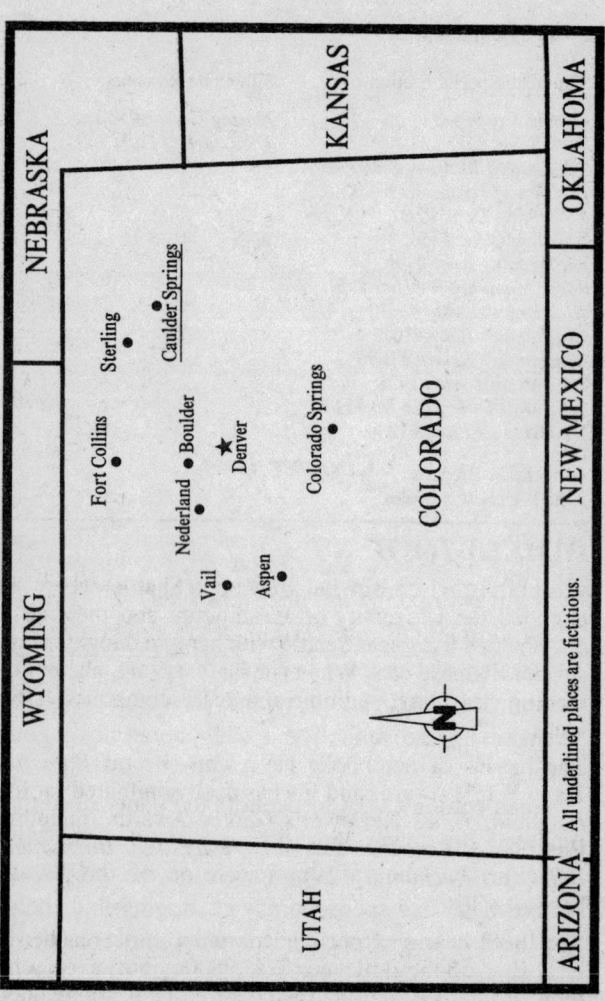

WYOMING

NEBRASKA

KANSAS

UTAH

COLORADO

Fort Collins

Sterling

Caulder Springs

Nederland • Boulder

Vail

Denver

Aspen

Colorado Springs

N

ARIZONA

NEW MEXICO

OKLAHOMA

All underlined places are fictitious.

Chapter One

Leah Randall was late. These days it seemed she was always running late for something.

Driving home from her job in town, she glared at her watch and pressed her foot down on the accelerator. Her old pickup rattled in protest, so she cranked up the radio for a song about love gone wrong.

Leah couldn't wait to peel off the panty hose that encased her lower torso like a second skin. Miss MacPherson, the spinster in charge of the library where Leah had spent the day cataloging and shelving books, was a stickler for what she considered proper attire. As soon as Leah got home, she planned to swap her straight navy skirt and tailored blouse for worn jeans, boots and one of her dad's old shirts. The week before, her only ranch hand had gone to live with his daughter in Seattle, leaving Leah to run the ranch alone. Thank goodness tomorrow was her day off from her paying job.

She'd had to stop and check on her mother before leaving town today and now it was nearly dusk. Another pickup, much newer than her own, was headed toward her on the highway. She stiffened as she recognized the gleaming late-model black Jimmy. Taylor Buchanan, the rancher from the spread bordering hers, raised a hand in greeting as the two rigs passed each other. Resolutely Leah stared straight ahead, both hands clenched tightly on the wheel.

Why did he bother? He must realize by now that she'd no more wave to a Buchanan than she'd say howdy to a coyote raiding her cattle. As far as she was concerned, one predator was just as bad as another.

Leah turned off the main highway and coaxed a little more speed from her old truck. This stretch of two-lane road was straight, flat and pretty much ignored by the local police. Darkness was falling rapidly now. As she slowed at her own dirt driveway, she switched on her headlights. If she hadn't, she might not have noticed what looked like a large bundle of dark clothes lying on the side of the road near a stand of aspens.

In the beam of her lights, the bundle turned over and a hand appeared.

Heart in her throat, Leah slammed on the brakes and the truck fishtailed in the dirt. Wishing that Duke, her dog, was with her, she grabbed a flashlight from the glove box and got out. A shiver of warning slid down her spine and she nearly wished Buchanan would drive by again, but the road remained stubbornly empty.

"Hello," she called out as she edged closer to the still form, unsure what she'd find. "Are you okay?"

As Leah approached, she glimpsed a smear of blood on the man's pale forehead and heard him groan. What was he doing out here alone? Where was his car?

Thinking with dismay of the empty rifle rack in her truck, she peered uneasily over her shoulder. Had someone dumped this man? Were they still around, watching her? A shiver crawled up her spine as she squatted beside him on the ground.

He groaned again and his eyes fluttered open. At least he was conscious.

"It's all right," she said automatically, playing the flashlight over his features. He appeared to be in his thirties, clean shaven, with short brown hair and a strong face that bore no other signs of injury. While Leah was wondering what to do, he squinted against the bright light and raised a protective hand to his eyes. His knuckles were scraped and swollen, as if he'd been in a fight.

"Damn, that's bright," he grumbled. "Can't you aim it somewhere else?"

Relieved he appeared coherent, Leah shifted the light away from his face. "Sorry," she said. "How do you feel?"

"Not sure," he muttered, then rolled over and struggled to sit up.

"Hey, not too fast," she warned him as he shut his eyes again and sank back down. "Your head's bleeding. You may have other injuries."

He frowned and touched his fingers to the ugly wound on his forehead, wincing when he made contact. He was very attractive, despite the disfiguring bump. His eyes were thickly lashed, his cheekbones were angled and his chin had a cleft. He looked vaguely familiar, but Leah didn't know him. You didn't forget a face like his.

"What happened to you?" she asked.

He glanced away. "Don't remember," he mumbled after a moment. "Who are you?"

Leah could certainly understand that he was shaken and confused. He might have been lying there unconscious for quite a while. "I'm Leah Randall," she volunteered. "Are you hurt anywhere else besides your head?"

Gingerly, he moved his arms and legs while she wondered whether she should be checking for broken bones. Surely he would be able to tell, and she had no medical training beyond the most basic. With dismay, she thought of her hungry animals and the chores that awaited her. Driving him back to town would add an hour and a half to her day, and that was assuming it was safe to move him. She didn't know much about head injuries. Perhaps it would be all right to take him to the house and call for help instead.

"Nothing broken," the man said, wincing as he flexed his battered hand.

While they were waiting for help to arrive, she could at least make him comfortable. The wind was coming up and he wasn't even wearing a jacket. Although his casual clothes were covered with dust, he looked too well dressed for a drifter.

With a muffled groan, he finally managed to sit up. "My head aches like hell."

"Were you on horseback?" Leah asked. "Were you thrown?"

He shook his head and then he swore under his breath.

"Where's your car?" she persisted. "How did you get out here?"

He peered into the darkness surrounding them. "I don't know."

Did he mean he didn't know where his car was or how he'd gotten here? It seemed pointless to grill him with questions. Let Sheriff Brody sort it out later.

Meanwhile, how was she going to get this man to the house? She couldn't lift him. He looked pretty solid, but if he could stand up, they should be able to manage. Leah was thin, but she was used to hard work. Her father had always said she was wiry and strong for her size.

Should she have insisted he lie still until the doctor came? Now that darkness had fallen, the temperature was dropping quickly. Leaving him here by the road didn't seem practical. Leah got to her feet and hoped she was doing the right thing. Maybe taking a stranger home wasn't smart, but she didn't have the time to stand around imagining all the scary things that could happen if she did. She'd always been a practical person, and this seemed like the practical thing to do.

"If we can get you in my truck, I'll drive you to the house," she told him. "We'll call for help from there. You'll want the doctor to look at your head."

He frowned again, his mouth taut, and she figured he must have a doozy of a headache. She was careful not to shine the light in his eyes.

"No doctor," he pronounced as she helped him to his feet. "I'll be fine."

Typical stubborn male. Leah was about to argue, but he swayed alarmingly. "Whoa there!" she exclaimed, sticking out a steadying hand. Even hunched over, he topped her by a head. "If you fall, I won't be able to catch you, so let's take it real slow."

Resolutely he steadied himself, feet braced wide like a newborn foal, while she hovered anxiously. "Okay?" she asked when he took a step.

A muscle twitched in his jaw. "Yeah. I can make it."

Leah meant to take his arm, but something held her back. He was awfully big and very male.

He must have sensed her hesitation. "I'm in no shape to make a pass," he said dryly.

"Of course not." Heat ran up her cheeks at being read so easily and she moved closer. "Lean on me."

Gingerly, he laid his arm across her shoulder. She'd been wrong. He was tall, but he was rangy rather than solid, with wide shoulders and long legs.

"What's your name?" she asked as they started walking.

"John."

She waited, but no more information seemed to be forthcoming. "Well, John," she said as they progressed slowly to the truck, "it looks as though that gash might need stitches. You're lucky Doc Hershaw still makes house calls."

"I don't want a doctor," he said again, pulling away from her as if to prove he could manage by himself.

Leah glanced at his clothes. His shirt looked new, his jeans weren't worn and he was wearing pricey boots, but that didn't mean he was flush. She knew plenty of ranch hands with fancy footwear and empty wallets.

"If you're worried about the bill, I'm sure you can work out something," she told him as he took two more lurching steps. "You local?" Just because she'd never seen him at the library in town didn't prove much. Most of the ranches in the area hired extra help this time of year. She couldn't compete with the wages they offered; that was one reason she hadn't yet found a replacement for Eli.

"No, I'm not from around here," John replied.

With a sigh, Leah circled his waist to steady him. When he swayed again, they both nearly went down.

"Sorry," he gasped. "I'm a little dizzy."

"Understandable." She took more of his weight and they moved forward. Their progress was slow, but finally they got to the truck, where he sagged against the fender. She pulled open the passenger door, pushed aside the junk on the seat and hovered nervously as he braced himself and took a couple of deep breaths. What the heck was she going to do if he fainted?

Finally he grabbed the door handle and put his foot on the running board. His head was down. She held her breath. Was he gathering his strength or praying for it?

The muscles in his arms bunched under his plaid shirt. As he climbed up, Leah lifted her hands to give him a boost and stared helplessly at the denim pulled tight across his compact rear end. Before she could figure out where to put her hands, he was safely in the cab.

"All set?" she asked, annoyed at herself for her temporary distraction. The poor man had been hurt;

the last thing he needed was a lonely female drooling over him. How pathetic.

His head bobbed in reply to her query. Carefully, she shut his door and circled the truck.

"I'd run you to town," she explained after she'd slid behind the wheel, "but my ranch hand quit and I've still got stock to feed." In the glow of the interior light, she glanced over to see that his head was resting against the back of the seat and his eyes were closed. His profile, starkly perfect, could have been lifted from an old coin.

"That's okay," he muttered, as if talking hurt his head. "Nice you stopped." He lapsed into silence, leaving Leah's curiosity unsatisfied as she tried to avoid the worst of the potholes. Despite her efforts, the truck bumped along like an old buckboard, forcing her to ease up on the accelerator until they were barely moving.

"Truck needs shocks," John mumbled.

"Needs a lot of things," she replied. The faded red pickup had been her father's. There was a Jeep out back, but it didn't run. Her mother had never learned to drive, so after his death Leah reluctantly sold the Mustang she'd owned since high school. There'd been no practical reason to keep it around, but she still missed that car.

"Your hired man quit," John said after a couple more minutes, opening his eyes and turning his head toward her. "You shorthanded?"

"I was shorthanded *before* Eli left," Leah admitted with a wry grin. "Now all I need is a few more hours in the day."

"I'm sorry to keep you from your work."

"Not your fault." What else could she say? Leah hated feeling selfish, but her time was stretched so darn thin that sometimes she felt like a rubber band—ready to snap. She worried about the ranch and worried about her mother, and now John had dropped in her path. What was she supposed to do with him until help showed up? She probably shouldn't leave him alone in the house. It wasn't that she had much to steal if he was inclined, or able, but with that head injury, he could pass out right on her couch. She sure hoped Doc Hershaw was available. If he was on a call at the other end of the county, she had no idea what to do.

The man sitting beside her was wondering a few things, too, like who the hell he was and how he'd gotten here. Wherever *here* was. He had no idea. He didn't even remember his name, although he'd told her the first thing that had popped into his head. John, as in John Doe. His wallet was gone; he'd already checked. Either he'd been robbed or it had fallen from his pocket.

The loss of memory yawned like a big black hole that threatened to swallow him up until there was nothing left. The harder he tried to remember anything at all, the more his head throbbed and the more panicky he became. Licking dry lips, he sneaked a glance at the woman, Leah. She was young, maybe late twenties, with straight blond hair and light-colored eyes. With a little care and different clothes, she could be pretty.

Not that her appearance mattered. He had enough problems of his own.

Trying not to moan out loud whenever she hit a bump, he speculated about what she'd do if she found out he was suffering from some kind of temporary amnesia. Probably call the local gendarmes. Being grilled by the cops when he had no answers for them was the last thing he needed to deal with at this point. He was exhausted and scared, and his gut told him they wouldn't be able to help.

Not that he needed anyone meddling in his business—or poking around in his head. He was used to handling things on his own. He might not know much, but somehow he knew that.

He thought back over how he'd acted since she first rescued him and what he'd told her. Damn little. Did she suspect anything? Probably not or she wouldn't be taking him home with her like a stray cat she'd found. It didn't sound as though she had three strong brothers or a husband to protect her, either, or she wouldn't be so worried about getting her stock fed.

He glanced at her sharply. She was taking a chance with him. He puzzled over that, wondering about her. Not everyone would have stopped to help, especially a woman all by herself. Did that make her a fool or a saint? And was he a good guy or a bad guy? He had no idea. How could you tell if you were a decent person?

He glanced at his sore knuckles. He'd hit someone. He couldn't remember who, or why, but he could recall the feeling of his hand smashing into flesh and bone. He struggled to picture a face, any face, and failed.

Fear bubbled up inside him. What if he was in some kind of serious trouble? He might still be in danger and he'd never know it. He could be putting this woman at risk, as well. Perhaps he'd had a fall-ing-out with someone, had fought with them and been left here. Nervously, he looked around. Then another thought chilled him. What if he was on the run, a fugitive from the law? Rejecting the idea as quickly as it took shape, he tried hard to penetrate the darkness surrounding his mind like a thick fog, but it expanded around him, threatening to suck him in. Pain speared his head and he was forced to give up, at least for now.

Until he remembered something, who he was and what had happened to him, he needed to keep a very low profile. The problem would be getting Leah Randall to cooperate.

His stomach lurched, sending bile into his throat and making him dizzy. He reached out a hand to the dash to steady himself and stared at his bloody knuckles. Was he a violent man?

"You okay?" Leah asked. "You feel sick? Try to hang on. We're nearly there."

He nodded tersely. "I'm fine." Well, it seemed he could lie if he needed. Somehow he'd have to persuade her not to tell anyone he was here until he figured out what was going on. So far she hadn't asked many questions, but he doubted her restraint would last. She must be wondering, and he'd better come up with a plausible story or she *would* get suspicious.

He'd figure out something, just as soon as his head stopped pounding.

They were approaching some buildings illuminated by the light from an overhead pole. For just an instant, he panicked and thought about taking her truck and leaving. He'd have to tie her up so she couldn't get to the phone.

What the hell had gotten into him? The whole idea was absurd. She'd stopped to help him. The idea of hurting this woman made his stomach roll more alarmingly than before, and he had to swallow hard to keep from disgracing himself.

His reaction gave him hope that he wasn't a hardened criminal, but it didn't rule out the possibility that he might have been involved in some kind of trouble. People got sucked into things they couldn't control. Again that feeling of helpless frustration washed over him. His hands shook. Quickly he clenched them at his sides, the right one aching sharply when he did and pain shooting through his head. He sensed that on the other side of the black void lay something he didn't want to face, but damned if he could get any kind of fix on what it was.

As the woman braked the truck, a black-and-tan dog ran into the driveway, barking noisily. The man started to open his door. The dog, a big fella with shepherd blood, caught his scent and bared its teeth.

"Duke!" she scolded. "Be a good boy."

Instantly, the dog circled around to her door, bushy tail wagging. A memory shimmered through John's head and was gone again before he could grasp it. Did he have a dog? Was that why he knew this one was part shepherd?

"Can you get out by yourself?" she asked him. "Duke won't hurt you."

"I'm okay." His head was throbbing badly now, nearly more than he could stand. If she saw his pain she'd insist on calling the doctor. Carefully, he eased himself out of the truck. Perhaps, if he could convince her he felt okay, she'd just let him bed down in the barn until morning. Surely his memory would return by then. He'd figure out what to do next and then he'd be out of here, thumbing if she couldn't give him a lift to town.

"Come inside," she urged. "I want to look at that wound under better light. Have you eaten? Do you want some coffee?"

Of course he couldn't remember when he'd eaten last, just knew he wasn't hungry. "No, thanks," he managed to reply through the pain that was rapidly turning into a red haze. "I'd take a glass of water and some aspirin, though."

She smiled, just a gentle curving of her lips. Her eyes were a light clear blue with no hint of gray. Despite his pounding head, he revised his opinion about her attractiveness.

"We'll take care of you." She led the way up the steps of the small farmhouse and opened the front door. John noticed it hadn't been locked and wondered why that surprised him. Did it mean he wasn't used to local customs? That he really wasn't from around here, just as he'd told her?

When she switched on a light in the small living room, another wave of dizziness nearly toppled him and he squeezed his eyes shut.

"Sit down here," she said, taking his arm and steering him toward a couch covered with a striped blanket. "I'll get you that water."

When Leah came back into the room with a brimming glass and the aspirin bottle, the couch was empty. She glanced around and saw John standing by the window near the telephone. He was pale, but at least the wound on his forehead hadn't started bleeding again.

"Did you want to use the phone?" she asked. He probably had family or someone who would worry when he didn't show up.

"No, thanks," he said through gritted teeth. His hands were braced on the small table and she noticed that he wasn't wearing a ring. "Look, if you'd just clean the wound and slap a bandage on it, I'd be grateful.'' His voice was low and strained. He sounded like a man nearing the end of his rope.

Leah handed him the glass and he drained half the water. ''It could need stitches, or you might have a concussion,'' she argued, reaching past him for the phone. ''Don't you want to report whatever happened to the sheriff?''

He wrapped his fingers around her wrist and she froze, realizing as Duke began to bark that she'd left him outside. Her gaze locked with John's. His eyes, she noticed irrelevantly, were hazel. Right now they were boring into hers.

''All I need is rest,'' he insisted.

Sudden fear trickled along her spine, but she refused to give in to it. Instead, she pulled away from him. ''Let me go!''

He released her instantly and stepped back. ''I'm sorry.'' He ducked his head. ''Look, I'm not up to dealing with questions and paperwork, not tonight. Waiting until morning won't make that much difference.''

Automatically, Leah handed him the aspirin. She wanted to argue further, but Duke had started to raise a ruckus outside, barking in earnest and scratching at the closed door. When she let him in, the dog plastered himself to her side. A low growl rose in his throat and the hair along his spine lifted as he stared at John. Murmuring softly, Leah petted his broad head.

Duke had been dumped at the end of her road two years ago, starving and beaten. She had nursed him back to health and now he was utterly devoted to her. "It's okay," she soothed, watching John as he gulped down several aspirin.

"I'm sorry," he repeated when he'd washed down the pills with the rest of the water. "I didn't mean to—" Cheeks stained a dusky red, he spread his hands helplessly. "I hope I didn't scare you."

As if she would admit it. "You didn't. Besides, Duke will tear you apart if you try anything." Good thing John couldn't know the dog was all teeth but no bite. Someone in his past had abused him. Even the barn cats terrified him. They stole his food from under his nose while he shook with fear. Leah could feel him trembling now, but the man didn't need to know that.

Her father's gun was in the drawer by her bed and the rifle was by the back door. She could probably get to one of them if she needed to, but she didn't think this man was really a threat—not the way he'd flushed with embarrassment after grabbing her wrist. Not the way he sank back down on the couch now, as pale as skim milk.

"I guess I can understand how you feel about calling the sheriff, but whoever hurt you is getting away. While I'm looking at your head, you'd better tell me exactly what happened," she said. "Can you make it to the bathroom? The light's better in there."

John followed her meekly and sat on the closed

toilet lid. The tiny room was crowded with the two of them and Duke all squeezed into it. The dog's presence lent her moral support, at least.

Gingerly, Leah cleaned the wound on John's temple with a wet cloth while he sat unmoving. As she washed away most of the blood, she was relieved to see the injury wasn't as bad as she'd first thought. Maybe he was right about the doctor. The area was swollen, but the damage appeared fairly minor. "It might leave a scar," she cautioned.

John made one of those macho snorts that indicated he was too tough to be concerned with such things. "Got any antiseptic?" he asked. "That and a bandage is all I need. And a decent night's rest. By morning I'll be fine."

"You still haven't told me what happened out there," Leah persisted. "Were you hitchhiking?"

She'd rested one hand on his wide shoulder as she cleaned his forehead. Before she moved it, she felt the muscles go rigid under her palm.

"Yeah, I was hitchhiking," he replied. As she rinsed out the cloth, he lapsed into silence.

"And then what happened?" she prompted, dabbing the wound with a cotton ball. Honestly, prying information out of him was like getting Duke to talk.

"Happened?" John echoed as she surveyed her handiwork.

"Yeah," she urged. "What happened next? How did you get from hitching a ride to lying in my driveway with a bump on your head?"

"Oh, that." He frowned. "We argued. He didn't want to take me any farther. When I got out of his truck I must have tripped, hit my head on a rock."

Leah gaped at him, the roll of tape in her hand nearly forgotten. "And he drove away?"

John shrugged. "Guess so."

Indignation flooded through her. "Well, you have to call and report him," she insisted as she taped a gauze pad on the cut.

"For what?" John demanded. "He gave me a ride. He let me out. What laws did he break?" His gaze was steady on hers and his eyes appeared to be evenly dilated. Did that mean he didn't have a concussion? She wasn't sure.

Before she could argue, he got to his feet and brushed past her. "Thanks for fixing me up," he said.

Leah trailed after him back into the living room. Suddenly Duke whined. He was standing in the kitchen with his front paws on the counter below the cupboard where she kept his canned food. Remembering the chores that still awaited her, Leah glanced at the old grandfather clock in the corner.

John must have noticed. "Look, if you'd just let me bed down in your barn tonight, I'd be much obliged. Before I leave in the morning, I'll help you out around here. You must have some work I could do to repay you, especially if you live alone."

The poor man must be exhausted, she realized

guiltily. No doubt what he needed most was rest, and she'd been playing twenty questions.

"I appreciate the offer," she replied, "but I really don't think you're going to feel like cleaning stalls tomorrow."

He shrugged. "Whatever needs doing, I can do," he insisted. "Maybe I could stick around for a few days, help you out."

"Isn't there somewhere you need to be?" Leah asked. And how was he going to get anywhere without a car? She supposed she could give him a ride to the bus station in town, but the idea of another pair of hands pitching in was sorely tempting. Maybe she could take him the day after, on her way to work, instead.

"I'm in no hurry," John replied, puzzling her. Perhaps he was just a rootless drifter, after all.

Duke whined again. Leah realized how late it was getting and how tired she was. It had been a long day and tomorrow would be no different. She searched John's face, wanting desperately to go along with what he'd suggested, but not sure she should. Perhaps she'd give Sheriff Brody a call when she got the chance, just to be on the safe side. It wouldn't hurt to rule out escaped convicts or missing mental patients. Not that John acted like either, but how did she know for sure?

"You look beat," he said quickly. "You wouldn't have to pay me wages or anything, just room and board for a few days. Like I said, I could stay in the barn, eat a couple cans of beans. How about it?'' He stuck out one big hand.

''Let's both sleep on it and see how you feel in the morning,'' Leah replied cautiously. Not wanting to appear rude, she put her hand in his. Immediately, his fingers tightened. She remembered how they'd felt wrapped around her wrist, but this time his touch was different. Warm, strong and reassuring. His gaze remained steady, as though he had nothing to hide. She looked into his eyes. There was a gold ring around each pupil. It reminded her of a halo. Now she was getting fanciful. Next she'd be looking for wings and thinking God had sent her a guardian angel to help with the chores.

Well, maybe John would feel more like talking about himself in the morning.

As he released her hand, his face relaxed into a grin for the first time. ''Fair enough.''

His smile was far from that of an angel, Leah thought distractedly. The last thing it evoked in her mind was heavenly thoughts. What was she getting herself into?

It seemed like hours later by the time Leah had John settled into the barn and she'd finished the chores. He'd offered to help, but she could see he was about to collapse, so she refused. He insisted he wasn't hungry, and when she took him a tray with soup and a sandwich later, along with an old jacket of her father's, he was sound asleep on the narrow cot in the tack room. For a moment she stood in the doorway, tray in hand, and watched him in the dim light from the passageway.

His face was in profile so the bandage on his forehead was hidden. He'd removed his shirt and his bare arms rested on the blanket she'd given him. They were muscular and tanned, as if he was used to working outside. Again Leah was tempted to accept his offer to stick around for a few days. The work was piling up and she had little time to do anything more than the basic necessities.

Deciding not to bother him with food, she set the tray down and backed silently out the door. If he woke up, the soup and the tea would be cold, but he might want the sandwich.

John watched through his lashes until she disappeared. Only when he couldn't hear her footsteps any longer did he open his eyes and glance at the tray she'd left. He knew he needed to eat, but food was the last of his concerns. Carefully he got to his feet and looked out the high window, watching her walk across the lighted ranch yard. Whistling to the dog, she disappeared into the house. The kitchen light winked out. After a few minutes, one went on at an upstairs window. A dark shape moved beyond the curtain. Feeling like a Peeping Tom, John shifted his attention to the yard.

Nothing about the scene seemed even remotely familiar. If he was a rancher, he didn't remember it. In the morning he'd make up some excuse to walk back to where she'd found him and look for his wallet. If he could find it, perhaps something inside, a photo or a phone number, would jog his memory. There might be someone he could call, someone who was wondering where he was. For now it was the only thing he could think to do.

Sitting back down on the cot, he glanced again at the tray. Ignoring the sandwich and the bowl of soup, he reached for the aspirin bottle she'd so thoughtfully provided and downed two more pills. He drained the cup of cooling tea and lay back down with a troubled sigh, intending to formulate some sort of plan. In minutes, oblivion covered him like a heavy blanket and he slept.

Chapter Two

Leah's alarm clock went off before the sun came up. Her room was lit only by the glow from the yard light when she crawled out of bed, but she didn't need even that as she opened drawers by touch and threw on her clothes. Yawning, she padded downstairs to let Duke outside. Once the stock was seen to, she could shower and get breakfast for both the dog and herself.

Leah wasn't a morning person, and she was starting the coffee when she finally remembered the man sleeping in her tack room. Hastily, she glanced out the window. The barn was still dark. In the yard, nothing moved.

Was John still asleep or had she dreamed the bizarre events of the night before? If he really did exist, how was he feeling this morning? Should she have insisted he see the doctor, talk to the sheriff? Perhaps she'd better make sure he hadn't lapsed into a coma. While she was at it, she might as well take him a cup of coffee, just in case he was conscious.

While it finished brewing, Leah raced back upstairs to brush her teeth and run a comb through her hair. She wasn't trying to impress anyone, she reasoned. It was just basic hygiene. John would be more interested in caffeine than in her appearance anyway.

She glanced down at her faded flannel shirt, started to unbutton it and decided she'd better draw the line somewhere. She had a ranch to run and there was no time in her schedule for primping.

When she got back downstairs, the coffee was ready. Cautiously, she sniffed the container of milk in the refrigerator. Wrinkling her nose in disgust, she poured it down the drain and hoped the man in her barn liked his java black. She slipped on her jacket, filled two mugs and headed outside.

When she stopped on the porch, pink was just bleeding into the eastern sky. The April air was cool, but not uncomfortably so. She filled her lungs with its freshness and then she took a bracing sip of coffee as she surveyed her domain. The barn begged to be painted and its roof was missing a few shingles. Some of the fence posts were starting to lean.

The dog ducked under the corral gate. Eventually he'd come back, wanting his breakfast and the reassurance of Leah's presence. Sometimes she envied him the simplicity of his needs.

Her thoughts turned to the man in her barn as curiosity and concern twisted together in her stomach. There was something about him she couldn't put a finger on, like a puzzle piece she knew was missing but couldn't identify.

Leah shook her head and the coffee sloshed dangerously. No, she was only being fanciful. He was a man who didn't like talking about himself, one entitled to his secrets. No more, no less.

Perhaps after a night's rest John would be more eager to tell his story to the law. Some people just didn't care for cops. Her own father had been that way, even though he and Sheriff Brody's predecessor had known each other since grade school. On more than one occasion, she remembered the patrol car dropping him off on a Friday night after he'd been drinking in town.

Now the old sheriff was retired to Florida and her father was dead. If not for the Buchanans, he might still be alive and her mother wouldn't be a prisoner of the world she'd created in her mind.

Yes, the Buchanans had a lot to answer for, all right—if not technically to the law or even to Leah, perhaps to a higher power who would mete out a fitting retribution for the lives they had damaged with their arrogance and greed.

Carefully, Leah set the coffee mugs on a post and slid open the barn door. Several horses poked their heads out of their stalls, ears pricked in her direction. A chestnut gelding named Star whinnied a greeting. In the shadows, a black-and-white cat disappeared behind some old crates as another, a big orange tabby, walked boldly over to Leah, its tail stuck up like a plume.

"Hi, Sassy." She shifted both mugs to one hand so she could reach down and scratch behind the cat's ears. Awareness shimmied through her and she looked up to see a tall figure leaning against the tack-room doorway, watching her. Startled, she nearly spilled the coffee.

John's arms were folded across his chest and he was wearing the jacket she'd left for him the night before. Its bulkiness made him look even bigger and more imposing than she remembered, while the bandage on his forehead and a blur of whiskers gave him the inexplicable appeal of a desperado. Leah had always found strays hard to resist, and John was no exception.

"Good morning," she said with a tentative smile. "How are you feeling?"

He straightened away from the door frame and rolled his shoulders. "I'm okay. Is that coffee?" He didn't walk like a man in pain as he sauntered toward her. "I swear I could smell it before I heard you coming."

Leah managed to keep her hand steady and pass him a cup without spilling it. "I hope you like it black and strong."

His full mouth tightened for an instant. "I'm sure I do," he drawled, puzzling her. He took a cautious sip and rolled his eyes. "Perfect. Thanks."

Leah flushed with pleasure. "I'll fix breakfast as soon as I have the horses turned out," she offered. Duke nudged her leg and she buried one hand in his fur as he wagged his tail. "Head hurt?" she asked John.

For an instant, his gaze clouded over. "Not much."

He certainly wasn't an effusive talker, she thought. "I'll change your bandage when we go back to the house. At least I don't have to go in to work today."

"Work?" he echoed, clearly startled. "I thought this was your ranch."

"I also have a part-time job at the library in town," she explained, "but today's my day off." Out of habit, she glanced at her watch. "I'd better get started."

John drained his coffee. "I'll help if you'll show me what to do."

She studied him for a moment over the brim of her mug. His color was better and he seemed to focus just fine. She wasn't about to turn down an extra pair of hands. He was looking around curiously and Leah wondered if he had any ranch experience.

"Have you worked with horses?" she asked. She boarded six head as well as her own three; she gave riding lessons to a couple of kids from town and the new wife of a neighboring rancher. The woman was from Chicago and had never been in a saddle before coming to Colorado.

Leah had a small herd of cattle, but horses were her first love. The money from lessons and boarding helped to cover expenses and to pay for her mother's care.

"A little," John said, but he didn't sound too confident as he walked over to where an old gelding was poking his head out of his stall. Immediately, Patches bared yellow teeth. John stopped in his tracks and then he gave Leah a sheepish glance.

"Does he bite?"

She had to smother a laugh. "Patches? Just carrots. Tell you what, I'll turn them out and you clean stalls." She pulled an extra pair of work gloves from her hip pocket and handed them to him. "Wheelbarrow and pitchfork over there." She pointed. "Clean shavings down at the end of the row. Compost heap outside." She explained what she wanted as he donned the gloves and flexed his bruised knuckles. No doubt they were still tender.

"When we're done here, I want to go back to where you found me and poke around a little," he said. "I must have dropped my wallet in the grass."

"I'll drive you," Leah replied. "Did you have a bag with you, too?"

"A bag?" He looked puzzled.

"Luggage? A change of underwear, perhaps?" she teased.

John flushed. "Oh, yeah. Sure."

She wondered why he looked so uncomfortable. Surely not because she'd mentioned underwear. Perhaps she'd read him all wrong and he *was* down on his luck, ashamed to admit he was traveling light. As if *she* were loaded and living in a mansion. She'd been forced to sell off some of her land to Buchanan to pay bills and she was still barely scraping by.

"What did your bag look like?" she asked as she entered the first stall and greeted Jewel, the black mare she had raised from a filly. Jewel had been blessed with showy white stockings, a blaze on her forehead and endless patience with beginning riders.

John was standing in the aisle. "Like a regular bag, I guess. But you don't have to go with me. I can walk."

"It's no trouble," Leah mumbled absently as she scratched Jewel under her forelock. She wondered if he'd really lost his wallet or someone had taken it and he just didn't want to admit it—some male pride thing she didn't understand.

"Some of my dad's clothes may fit, if you need them," Leah offered. Might as well get some use from the stuff she'd never bothered to dispose of. John was close to the same height as her dad, but any resemblance between the two men stopped there. Her father had been thicker around the middle and not as broad through the shoulders. Drinking had left its mark on his face, as well, while John's appeared to be weathered only by sun and wind.

"Won't your father mind?" he asked as she

opened the outside stall door and stepped back. Jewel blew out a breath and tested the air, nostrils quivering, before ambling past Leah.

Only then did John enter her stall. Not a ranch hand, Leah decided. "My father died a few years ago," she said.

"I'm sorry." John's voice sounded genuinely regretful. "Was he ill?"

Sudden tears filled her eyes and she pretended to fiddle with the latch on the door. Funny how much the loss still hurt, especially when there had been so many unresolved issues between them. Their family hadn't been the Brady Bunch, that was for sure. "He was riding dirt bikes with a friend. His flipped over on him and he died instantly."

John was gazing at her intently, as if he was really interested. "At least I was already grown up when it happened," she added.

Something flickered in his eyes and then was gone. "Did that make it easier?"

"No, of course not. It's just that I got to spend more time with him, that's all." She was about to ask about his family when he turned away abruptly and headed for the wheelbarrow. Maybe he didn't have a cowboy's ambling gate, but watching him move was still pleasurable.

"I'd better get started or the boss will be after me," he called back over his shoulder, making Leah wonder if he'd been aware of her scrutiny. Frowning, she exited Jewel's stall and greeted Candy.

John was definitely a hard worker, she thought later as they piled into her truck. While she'd fed and watered the horses and the barn cats, he'd finished mucking out stalls. If his head or his bruised hand bothered him, he never complained. Once Leah had suggested he take a break, but he'd only shot her a disgusted look as he disappeared outside with the loaded wheelbarrow.

After she'd checked on him once and told him to holler if he needed her, she hadn't wanted to hover and make him feel uncomfortable, so she'd purposely left him alone. On his trips to the compost heap he'd been whistling tunelessly, and once, when she was playing with Hailey's foal, she'd heard a muffled curse from inside the barn. Since it hadn't been followed by a shout for help, she'd stayed where she was. With his assistance, the morning chores had been done in nearly half the time it usually took her.

"Are you sure the guy who gave you the ride didn't drive off with your bag?" she asked as Duke jumped into the back of the pickup and they headed down the road.

John shrugged. "Didn't think he did. Sure is pretty country around here. Did you grow up on this ranch?"

Leah followed his gaze as they bumped along toward the main road. It had been quite a while since she'd really taken the time to appreciate her surroundings. Usually all she noticed was what needed to be done. Today the sky above was nearly empty of color, but the land that rolled up to meet it was finally greening over. Its palette was changing from the dead browns and faded tans of the season past and starting to reflect instead the vibrancy of new spring growth. Along the road, dark purple prairie crocus bloomed.

This last winter in eastern Colorado had been an especially harsh one, whose end she'd been glad to see. Feed for the stock had cost more than she'd expected and she was looking forward to summer, even though the warmer weather would mean more work than ever. She'd need permanent help before then.

"Except for college I've always lived here," she replied when she realized John was still waiting for an answer. "My grandfather bought this land." Some of her fondest memories were of the time she'd spent with him before he died in a blizzard. Much as she'd tried, her relationship with her father had never been as close. Perhaps if he'd lived—

"Where did you go to school?" John interrupted her thoughts as he shifted in the seat and rearranged his long legs. Suddenly the cab seemed cramped as it never had before, even when there were three people crowded inside.

"Colorado State up in Fort Collins. I went for nearly three years." A whole new world had opened up for her then, but being called back home before she was ready had been a painful necessity—one beyond her control.

"Why did you quit?" He narrowed his eyes and

turned to look out his side window. "Sorry. That's really none of my business."

Leah didn't mind telling him. Except for the patrons who came into the library, she didn't get to talk to people all that often, and she realized now just how much she missed the human contact.

Her friends were married or scattered. Her social life was a big fat zero, and most of her time was spent alone here at the ranch, talking to animals that didn't talk back.

"It's okay," she said. "You aren't being nosy. I quit college when my dad died. He was a bullfighter. A rodeo clown," she elaborated when John looked puzzled. "I always meant to go back for my degree, but I couldn't leave Mom here by herself." She waved one hand in a vague gesture.

Despite her efforts, Leah hadn't been able to fill even a small part of the hole her dad's death had left in her mother's life, she thought sadly.

"Where's your mom now?" John asked.

"She lives in town." Leah didn't elaborate. Being unable to cope with what her mother had become was one more failure on Leah's part. "I don't know," she concluded. "Maybe I'll still go back to school someday." It wasn't as though her mother would miss her visits.

John must have sensed that the subject was a painful one. "What was your major in school?" he asked.

"Medieval history. I loved learning about the people and their customs, their living conditions, the challenges and the hardships they dealt with. It's all so fascinating. I wanted to teach. I thought—'' She caught herself abruptly. ''Sorry. I didn't mean to go on like that.''

''You thought what?'' he asked. ''Tell me.''

Leah squirmed in the seat. Why had she brought this up? ''I thought I could make history interesting,'' she muttered, her gaze fixed firmly on the road she knew like the back of her hand. ''It can be so much more than just a dry subject in a textbook.'' She tucked a strand of hair behind her ear. ''That's all.'' She stopped the truck where she'd found him the evening before, wishing she'd kept her mouth shut.

''I'll bet you'd make a good teacher,'' John said as he opened his door.

Even though he couldn't know that with any certainty, his approving words gave her a jolt of pleasure. ''I work at the library now,'' she explained. ''But without a degree, I'm just a clerk. It's a pretty small branch and the head librarian is very traditional.'' That was putting it mildly. Miss Mac-Pherson saw no reason for change and she distrusted modern technology. The fax machine the district had sent was still sitting in its original box. Leah thought of her boss as a speed bump in the information highway.

She shut off the engine. Duke jumped down from

the bed of the truck and began nosing through the grass. Too bad he was no bloodhound.

Leah got out and John did the same. "So your boss looks at progress as a tool of the devil, huh?" he guessed, shoving his hands in his pockets and hunching his shoulders against the wind that had sprung up.

Leah nearly laughed out loud. "You got it. She fought against the new computer system and she doesn't think libraries should clutter their shelves with modern gimmicks like video tapes and CDs. I'm not sure she even approves of magazines."

His eyes crinkled at the corners when he smiled and then his pupils darkened as he continued to look down at Leah. Her mind went blank and the silence between them stretched awkwardly until she was finally able to glance away and break the spell.

"Now, what color is your wallet?" Slightly breathless, she studied the ground around them. Anything that small could easily be hidden in the tall grass.

He didn't answer, so she looked back up at him. He hadn't moved and he was frowning.

"The wallet?" she repeated. "Black? Tan? I'd be more likely to spot it if I knew what to watch for."

"You don't have to do this," he replied. "I know you're busy. Why don't you go on and I'll just walk back to the house. I'm not an invalid."

"No one said you were, but four eyes are better

than two," Leah replied. "That's what my mother always said."

"Interesting." John's tone was dry. "If you insist on staying, why don't you look over by the main road?"

Obviously he wasn't a man who accepted help readily. She could understand that. Since her father's death, she'd come to examine an outstretched hand with a dose of skepticism herself. To give John some space, she wandered in the direction he'd suggested, pausing to kick at a clump of grass. Some men didn't pay much attention to details like color, she reasoned. He could even be color-blind.

They'd been searching for ten minutes or so when she glimpsed something in an area of tall grass near a ditch. It was a navy blue duffel bag and it didn't appear to have been there very long. She picked it up and waved it triumphantly.

"Hey, does this look familiar?" she called out.

She thought John would be pleased with her discovery, but his face was grim as he hurried over. Squatting down, he unzipped the bag. She glimpsed some clothes, neatly folded, and a shaving kit. Too bad. She rather liked the soft blur of whiskers on his cheeks.

"I just wanted to make sure everything was here," he said finally as he closed the bag back up. "Thanks."

"No problem," Leah told him.

He thanked her again and tossed the bag into the

truck. They resumed the search for his wallet, moving in ever-widening circles. Leah found several beer bottles, a rusted rake and an old slipper, but that was all. Eventually John straightened and stretched as if he were loosening the kinks from bending over too long, then walked toward the truck.

"Are you giving up?" Leah called. Duke trotted over to her side.

"I think we've wasted enough time," John replied. He sounded disappointed.

"If your wallet fell from your pocket, it can't have wandered far," Leah argued as she joined him beside the truck. She'd lost her purse once, at school, and felt as though a part of her were missing until it was returned, miraculously intact.

"Maybe someone else picked it up," John said.

"Since last night? This isn't Times Square in New York City," Leah said, wondering why she was so reluctant to give up. She was getting hungry, and she still had to ride out and check the cattle before the day was over.

John's stomach gave a low rumble. "Didn't you say something earlier about breakfast?" He kicked at a clump of weeds with the toe of his boot.

Leah wondered once again if his wallet had been stolen. But why would he go through the charade of looking for it? Nothing about him added up. She shrugged philosophically. Well, it was his loss and his business. "Yes, I did promise to cook," she replied, signaling Duke, who jumped in the back of the truck. "If you're through looking, let's go." John had worked hard in the barn; he must be starving. She certainly was.

They got back in the truck and headed up the road to the house, John holding the duffel bag on his lap. Luckily Leah had stopped at the store in town a couple of days ago. Except for the milk that had soured, her larder was fully stocked with provisions. From her mother she had learned to cook the plain food her father favored and plenty of it. John might not find it exciting, but neither would he starve.

Slowly, he followed her into the house, not sure what she expected him to do or how much help he would be in the kitchen. To his relief, his offer of assistance was politely turned down. Duke, who had come inside with them, watched him from across the room, but he ignored John's cautious overture of friendship.

"Maybe I'll take my things out to the barn while you're busy," John suggested, eager to search the bag for clues. He hoped she wouldn't tell him not to bother, that he wasn't staying. To help her decide she couldn't get along without him, he'd worked his butt off earlier, even though his head had started to throb dully and he'd had no real clue what to do until she showed him.

What if she still told him to leave? Where would he go? Perhaps he should throw himself on her mercy, tell her the truth.

No, she'd want to call the sheriff and he wasn't

ready for that. He'd been convinced that when he woke up this morning his memory would have magically returned and this bizarre nightmare would be over. Instead, except for a few vague images that disappeared before he could focus on them, his life was still one big blank. Perhaps a more thorough search of the bag would yield something, anything, to trigger a glimmer of recognition.

Leah had been rattling around in the kitchen, measuring flour into a mixing bowl while he stood by awkwardly. Now she glanced up and wiped her hands on a faded towel. "If you'd like to shower, you're welcome to use the bathroom here in the house," she said with a little smile. "I'm sure you've noticed the one in the barn doesn't have hot water. Dad's knowledge of plumbing only went so far."

John scratched his chin and ran his fingers over the stubble that covered his cheeks. Funny that he could remember how good a hot shower felt, but not whether he'd ever had a beard—or how long he'd been wearing the clothes he had on.

"I'd like that," he said, "if you're sure you don't need my help here."

Leah brushed past him and headed toward the bathroom. "I move faster alone. I'll get you some towels. When you're done, I'll change your bandage."

John wasn't about to argue as he followed her and stopped in the bathroom doorway. As long as she didn't tell him to leave, she could climb in the shower with him and wash his back if she had a hankering.

The idea caused a rush of heat that wasn't helped by the sight of her bending over to get towels from a cabinet. All morning he'd been conscious of her as she took care of her horses. The sound of her voice as she crooned to them had drifted through the open window like a siren's song. Every time he wheeled a load of manure out to the compost pile, he got a glimpse of her moving around the corral with a simple athletic grace that was surprisingly erotic.

Until he got his memory back, he had no business thinking about her like that. He might be married, with a family. Right now some woman could be worried sick about him. Besides, if Leah realized the direction his thoughts were taking, she'd probably have Duke run him off the ranch.

Preoccupied, John stepped into the tiny bathroom, remembering only when it was too late how crowded it felt with the two of them squeezed in there together. Before he could beat a retreat, Leah eased by him. Their bodies brushed and John put out a hand to steady her. It closed on her upper arm and she froze. Her warmth soaked into his palm and he let her go reluctantly. He started to thank her, but his voice was hoarse and he had to clear his throat.

"I'll start breakfast," she said, sounding breathless, as if she'd been running. Had he spooked her? She didn't strike him as the nervous type.

"I won't be long." John let her go, shutting the

door firmly behind her, and turned eagerly to the bag he'd brought with him. Sitting down with it on his lap, he closed his eyes and breathed a wordless prayer. Slowly, heart pounding, he peeled open the zipper. Impatiently he dug out jeans that looked identical to the pair he was wearing and several western-cut shirts patterned in a variety of blue-and-white checks and plaid. For all he remembered, he'd never seen any of them before in his life. Neither the labels nor the sizes rang a bell. He might as well have been looking at the possessions of a stranger.

Discouraged, he dug deeper, hoping for a prescription bottle or some papers bearing his name. The shaving gear was generic, the underwear a common brand. He held up a faded gray T-shirt with a logo on the front in purple script. U Dub Dawgs. What the hell did that mean? Staring hard, he tried to open his mind. Hell, he couldn't even remember wearing the shirt. Thrusting it aside, he pulled out several pair of socks and noticed that one had a sizable lump in the toe.

When he shook it, a wad of bills fell into his palm. He counted them, hands trembling, and was relieved to discover he was nearly a thousand dollars away from dead broke. Dividing the money, he returned part of it to the sock, which he rolled back up and tucked into the bag, and shoved the rest into the back pocket of the jeans he'd set aside to wear. Refusing to speculate on how or where he'd gotten so much cash, he resumed his search. From an inside pocket he pulled out a folded baseball cap. It was blue and the word "Mariners" was embroidered across the front above crossed baseball bats. Frowning, he studied the design carefully.

Apparently he was a sports fan of sorts. Perhaps a newspaper would tell him what he wanted to know, unless the Mariners were some obscure high school team. A tag dangled from the cap, but to his disappointment, all it contained was the price. A souvenir? A going-away gift? Shaking his head, he put the hat back in the bag.

When he checked the inside pocket again, his fingers brushed something round and hard. He pulled out a ring. It was silver, with a modern design and a smooth black stone in the center. John narrowed his eyes, but the memories did not come rushing back. He was about to slip the ring on his finger when he thought to check inside the band. There, in tiny script, was engraved, To J.B. Love, M.B.

J.B. Maybe his name really was John. Or Joe, Jason, Jeremy or Jim. The possibilities were too numerous to consider.

And what about the other initials? Same last name? A wife? Was he married? If so, why wasn't he wearing a wedding band? Carefully, he examined his left hand for any sign of recent adornment. There was no faint dent, no mark, no tan line. Hardly conclusive, though. Lots of men didn't wear rings.

Was it possible he could have forgotten so completely any woman with whom he shared his life and his heart? A woman he'd chosen to love and to cherish? He didn't think so, not him. That kind of feeling would be too ingrained to be wiped out so completely. Absently, he slipped on the ring, working it over the bruised knuckle of his right hand. It fit perfectly. More important, it felt right.

He tipped back his head, blinking away the sudden film of moisture, and curled his fingers protectively. He felt as though he'd been given back a tiny part of himself.

John sucked in a deep, trembling breath, his faith renewed, and then he heard Leah's voice from beyond the closed door as she scolded Duke for something. Immediately, John became aware of time passing. Fumbling, he put down the bag, turned on the shower and stripped off his clothes.

Chapter Three

In the kitchen, Leah had been fixing breakfast with one ear cocked toward the bathroom until she heard the water go on in the shower. After the juvenile way she'd bolted earlier, John probably thought she was nuts. Arm still tingling from the touch of his hand, she hadn't slowed down until she reached the kitchen. She'd opened the refrigerator door, cheeks burning, and stared blindly at its contents until the ancient motor kicked on in protest.

What was wrong with her, anyway? she wondered now as she popped biscuits into the oven and set the timer. There was a naked, wet, perfectly gorgeous man in her bathroom, the first male to use the facilities since her no-good ex-husband had run off more than a year ago. No reason for Leah to come unglued.

Automatically, she turned over the strips of frying bacon and adjusted the heat beneath the pan. She knew nothing about John but his first name, she reminded herself as she broke eggs into a bowl. He could be an escaped convict. Even worse, he could be married.

Leah put the bowl aside and reached for the phone. The least she could do was call Sheriff Brody and see if there were any fugitives loose in the area. As far as the other was concerned, if she wanted to know John's marital status, she'd have to go to the source.

When John opened the bathroom door, letting out a cloud of steam, the aroma of frying bacon made his stomach growl in response. How long had it been since he'd eaten a decent meal? It was just one more question whose answer eluded him.

When he padded out in stocking feet to drop his bag by the door, Duke was lying under the kitchen table and Leah was hanging up the phone. He hadn't heard it ring, and he wondered who she had called. Before he could think of any casual way to ask, she gave him a guilty smile. Had she been telling someone about him, or was he just being paranoid?

"Feel better?" She didn't wait for a reply as she went to the stove and began dividing up fried potatoes and scrambled eggs onto two plates. Without thinking, John grabbed some silverware from the drying rack in the sink and set the table.

"I feel more human," he replied, running a hand

over his wet hair. "Thanks for letting me use the shower."

"No problem." Leah added bacon to the heaping plates and put them on the table. She didn't mention the phone call and he could think of no way to bring it up. Well, if the law was on its way, John would know soon enough. In the meantime, he might as well fill his belly.

"Anything else I can do?" he asked.

She studied the table for a moment. "I'm out of ketchup." She sounded apologetic.

"I can manage without it." Ketchup was the least of his concerns.

She tucked a strand of hair behind her ear. "Okay, then. Let's eat." She didn't look like a woman who'd just learned she was harboring a dangerous felon.

Without thinking, John held out a chair for her. Surprise flitted across her face and her cheeks turned pink. Ducking her head, she sat down with a muttered thanks.

"Looks good," he said gruffly, to cover the sudden awkwardness between them. There was juice, coffee, butter and honey, as well as the two steaming plates and a basket of biscuits. At least he had no trouble identifying the names of other everyday items.

For the next few minutes, neither of them spoke. John's pleasure in the meal was marred only by the knowledge that he had no idea what he usually ate or what his favorite foods were. Judging how good the bacon tasted, he was no vegetarian. Spreading butter and honey on a biscuit, he couldn't picture a single other meal he'd eaten, neither circumstances nor location. The black hole yawned as wide and deep as ever.

"It's delicious," he managed to say between mouthfuls. Once he started eating, it was all he could do to keep from shoveling the food in with both hands. Finally Leah sat back, plate empty, and sipped her coffee. As he broke open a second biscuit and buttered it, he noticed her watching him over the rim of her mug. Downing half the biscuit in one bite, he braced himself for the inquisition he suspected was coming next.

"That's an attractive ring," she said. "I didn't notice it before."

"It was in my bag," he replied warily.

Leah pushed back her chair. "When you're done eating, let me check your bandage."

Feeling as though he'd been granted a reprieve, John washed down the rest of his biscuit with the last of his coffee. Then he followed her meekly, sitting once again on the closed toilet seat while she took supplies from the medicine cabinet.

She was humming something under her breath, a catchy tune he didn't recognize. He tried to remember other melodies, but his mind stayed stubbornly blank.

"What are you humming?" he finally asked.

"Goodness, you aren't a country music fan, are

PAMELA TOTH 55

you?'' she retorted. "It's called 'Achy Breaky Heart' and it was on the charts forever.''

"Oh, sure, I just forgot,'' he said, even though the title was no more familiar than the tune itself. Perhaps she was right and he wasn't a fan. Would he ever remember what kind of music he did like? Or anything else? And what if he never did? How long could he avoid contacting the authorities for help? And why did the idea make his stomach tense? Someone out there might be worried about him.

"Does your head still hurt quite a bit?'' she asked as she turned around.

Something of his feelings must have shown on his face. "Nah. I just don't like being fussed over,'' he grumbled. His legs were spread and she was standing between his knees. Staring straight at the loose shirt that covered her breasts, he found himself speculating about them.

Were they small and round, like firm apples, or plump, soft ovals? The kind that settled into a man's palms, begging to be shaped by his fingers? Tipped by velvety pink nipples that tasted as sweet as candy, or brown ones that drew up tight and tart like berries?

Eyes shut, John shifted uncomfortably on the toilet seat. Not the best thoughts to be having with her so near he could reach out and—

"Ouch!'' His eyes flew open.

Leah was holding the bandage she'd just ripped from his forehead in one motion. Had she guessed his thoughts?

"Best way to do it," she explained, leaning even closer to examine the gash. "No point in prolonging the agony." She was pouting with concentration, her mouth soft and full—and too damn close for his peace of mind. There was an intriguing little hollow above the bow of her upper lip. While he stared, the tip of her pink tongue appeared.

John nearly groaned aloud. Her scent filled his head, sunshine and leather with a hint of lemon that might have been either soap or her shampoo. Shifting his attention, he peered right down the neck of her shirt. Luckily for his sanity, all he could see was a little skin and part of her bra strap. Plain white and serviceable, he guessed.

He was wondering just what she'd do if he put his hands on her waist and pressed his face to the front of her shirt, when she must have noticed his silent scrutiny. Abruptly, she stepped backward and bumped into the open bathroom door.

"You okay?" He shot out a hand to steady her.

"Fine, just fine." She drenched a gauze pad with antiseptic and held it out to him. "I think you can finish this yourself."

By the time he'd slapped a bandage on the gash, which had already scabbed over, and gotten a firm grip on his self-control, Leah was leaning against the kitchen counter with a mug of fresh coffee.

"I think it's time you answered a few questions," she announced before he could think of anything to say. "Don't you?"

Normally, Leah didn't consider herself a nosy woman, but there was something she couldn't put her finger on about John—something that just didn't add up. He wasn't like the men who'd come around in the past seeking work. Surely, if he was going to stay at her ranch, she was entitled to a few facts.

"What do you want to know?" he asked warily.

"Your last name?"

"Brown," he said quickly, perhaps too quickly.

She could hardly call him a liar on some vague hunch. "Where are you from, John Brown?" she persisted.

He frowned. "Here and there, I guess." He must have been able to tell from her expression that she wasn't satisfied with that. "I was born on the coast, but we moved a lot."

There was more she wanted to know, but he looked like a man who was ready to bolt. Perhaps he wasn't as tightly controlled as he wanted her to think. A shiver went through her, but it wasn't fear. Curiosity, surely, and a reluctant interest she was doing her best to ignore.

"Look, I just don't like talking about myself," he said, spreading his hands. "If you want me to leave, just tell me."

It was the last thing she expected him to say. "No, that's okay. I understand." Many of the men who drifted in for a few weeks or a season and then moved on were reluctant to answer questions. Perhaps John *was* like all the rest and she didn't want to see it. Maybe there were things in his past that he didn't like thinking about. As long as he was willing to help her out for a few days, who was she to insist he dredge them up?

He continued to stare down at her and a muscle jumped in his cheek. "What do you want me to do next?"

She had told the sheriff she was thinking about hiring a drifter. He'd asked if the man had given her any references. When she'd admitted that he hadn't, Sheriff Brody had tried to dissuade her. That didn't work, so he had offered to come out and look the man over for her. Leah still wasn't sure why she'd declined his offer, but between Duke and her dad's guns, she figured she could take care of herself.

John was standing with his hands on his hips, waiting expectantly. She'd needed help running the ranch and fate had brought it to her in the form of an attractive, reasonably healthy male who seemed willing to work. She'd be a fool to turn him away.

"Do you still want to hang around for a few days?" she asked. "I can't pay much, but I could give you room and board if you don't mind bunking in the stable."

Some of the visible tension went out of him. "That suits me fine, but I wouldn't take your money, anyway." He touched a finger to the bandage on his forehead. "I owe you for rescuing me."

"Someone else would have stopped if I didn't." They both knew that once darkness fell it would have been difficult, if not impossible, to see him. "Anyway, I'll toss in a few more hot showers," she offered, wondering if she was doing the right thing or making a terrible mistake. "And more plain cooking."

"Nothing wrong with your cooking and the deal sounds good to me." He shifted his weight from one leg to the other and she realized she'd been staring.

"Anything else?" he asked.

"Not for now." Leah began clearing the table, gratified when John pitched in. Her father had never helped in the house. He'd considered it woman's work, although Leah remembered her mother helping plenty with *his* manly duties. "We need to check on the cattle today," she told John as he carried their plates to the kitchen counter. "Do you ride?"

Feeling trapped, John set the plates down with care. They looked old, with flowers around the border, and he'd hate to break any. He was painfully aware that she was waiting for an answer to what should have been a simple question. He could say no, just to be safe, but something inside him refused to back away from the challenge.

He decided to compromise. "It's been a while. I don't know how much I remember."

"Don't worry," Leah said cheerfully as she stacked dishes in the sink. "That's something you never forget."

John choked back a bitter laugh. If she had any

idea just how much he *had* forgotten, she'd probably decide he was crazy and insist that he leave.

"The dishes can wait, but we'd better take some sandwiches with us." She put the perishables back into the refrigerator. "We'll be gone for several hours."

"No problem." John was hoping he'd hold up. At least he seemed to be in decent shape. The work he'd done in the barn had been easy enough. After his shower he'd noticed in the bathroom mirror that his stomach was flat and he carried no flab. Maybe he'd still be able to walk after several hours on horseback.

"Why don't you saddle the horses while I pack us a lunch?" Leah suggested.

What if he had no idea how to do that? "I'll make the sandwiches while you saddle the horses," he countered. "They're used to you. Just show me where the fixings are."

Leah gave him an odd look, but she didn't argue. Instead she pulled a loaf of bread from the drawer and a grocery bag from a cupboard. "Bologna and cheese in the fridge, lettuce in the crisper. Chips and cookies in the pantry." She glanced around. "I don't like mustard. Oh, throw in a couple cans of soda, too."

John had already grabbed a knife. "Mayo?" he asked, holding up the jar. Startled, he realized that he didn't like mustard, either.

"Sure," Leah replied, obviously unaware of his breakthrough discovery. "I'll see you outside."

A few minutes later, John walked out to where she was waiting with two of the horses he'd seen earlier, both saddled and ground-tied. One was black and the other was such a light gray that it was nearly white. Duke was sitting on the ground with his tongue lolling out and his ears pricked. The dog's gaze never left John, making him wonder if he was being sized up as a possible meal or just someone who bore close scrutiny. Clearly the truce John had attempted to forge with a piece of bacon slipped under the table at breakfast had been a temporary one.

Leah had donned a dusty black Stetson, and when she saw John, she held out an equally disreputable brown one.

"You'll need this," she said as he handed her the lunch he'd packed.

Wondering whether he should have grabbed the baseball cap from his bag, John plopped the hat on his head and tugged experimentally on the brim. It felt surprisingly comfortable. He realized he'd approached the horse she'd indicated without a qualm, automatically raising his hand for an introductory sniff.

He was barely aware of Leah telling him that the gray was named Candy, and except for a trot like a bad road, he was an easy ride. The gelding blew his warm breath on John's hand and a curtain parted in his mind. Relief flooded him. It was all he could do to keep from falling to his knees and kissing the ground.

He could ride. The knowledge was there, even if the memory wasn't. He had no idea how he could be so certain, but he was. A wad of emotion rose in his throat, threatening to choke him. To give himself a moment for composure, he turned his back to Leah and adjusted the stirrups with easy familiarity.

"Looks as though you remember a little bit," she commented, dividing the sandwiches and cans of soda between her saddlebags.

"Like you said," he agreed, "some things you don't forget."

Leah's thoughts scattered. If he were to smile like that more often, she'd be in big trouble. Dismayed, she gathered up Jewel's reins and swung onto the horse's back. When John mounted up, Candy took a couple of side steps in token protest. John settled him down with a few softly spoken words and then looked at Leah expectantly.

Wearing the Stetson she had loaned him pulled low over his eyes, he reminded her of one of the old sepia photographs she'd seen in a book on western history. All the man needed was a handlebar mustache and a six-shooter strapped to his hip to complete the romantic image.

"What's wrong?" he asked, shattering her daydream.

"Nothing." Leah called to Duke, who danced with excitement, avoiding her horse's legs. Jewel ignored him.

''We've wasted enough time.'' Leah was irritated without knowing why. ''Let's head out.''

Leah had been worried that John might not be able to keep up with her. If it truly had been a while since he was on horseback, he'd be sore later, but for now he rode as easily as if he spent a lot of time in the saddle.

''It's beautiful country,'' he said after they rode through a gate and Leah shut it carefully, leaving the ranch buildings behind them. ''You're very lucky.''

''Why do you say that?'' she asked. The last thing she'd felt lately, with her killer schedule and endless frustrations, was lucky.

''I have the impression that you have a good sense of who you are.'' His head was tipped back as he watched a magpie fly overhead.

Maybe she didn't much like who she was, Leah protested silently. Maybe she would have liked to trade places with someone else, someone with no responsibilities, no bills, no unfinished family business. But she couldn't say that to a man who didn't appear to be concerned with any of those things, a man who seemed to have neither roots nor responsibilities—or at least none he was willing to talk about. ''Doesn't everyone know who they are?'' she countered instead. ''Don't you?''

His gaze flicked away from hers. For a few moments, the only sounds were the swish of the grass, the muffled thud of horses' hooves and the jingle of their bridles. Leather creaked as he shifted in his saddle.

"I guess I thought I did once," he replied when she'd almost given up on a response. He sounded wistful, even sad. "Now I have no idea who I am."

"Who do you want to be?" She slowed so they were riding abreast. For some reason she couldn't understand, his answer was important. She was disappointed when he shrugged.

His grin was crooked. "I don't really know."

At that moment she spotted a group of cows and their calves. Her chance to ask more was lost as the cattle saw them and began to drift away.

"Damn," Leah exclaimed. "I was hoping to keep this simple." She motioned to Duke, who trotted off to the right.

"What do you want me to do?" John asked.

Without taking her gaze off the cattle, Leah gestured with her arm. "Circle to the left, but don't run at them. I just want a quick look."

When John started off in a bone-jarring trot, she nearly smiled. Well, she'd warned him about Candy's gait. She returned her attention to the cows that were milling nervously. With the fence behind them, they had nowhere to go except past her. To Leah's relief, they stayed put. Riding in close, she could see that all five heifers and their calves appeared healthy. Wounds from dehorning and castration at the recent roundup looked clean. She heaved a sigh of relief. With an operation as small as hers, every animal was important, every loss a big one.

"Looking good," she told John. "Let's move on." They inspected several more groups of varying sizes, checking fence in between, and then John spotted a single cow in the distance.

"Antisocial?" he asked.

Leah bit her lip. The cow appeared to be alone. "Perhaps the calf is just resting, but I need to find out for sure. They're awfully close to the bog."

A couple minutes later, Leah's worries were confirmed. The calf was stuck in the deep mud churned up by dozens of hooves at the edge of the watering hole, but at least it was still alive. Quickly she dismounted, one eye on the cow. Keeping the calf between them, she assessed the situation. The calf must not have been trapped for long; it didn't appear to be too weak as it bawled in fright.

Stepping carefully into the smelly, slick mud, Leah tugged on the calf with her gloved hands. The animal rolled its eyes and bawled again. When pulling on it didn't work, she glanced at John, who was already half out of his saddle.

"I could use your help." Her boots sank deeper and she knew that staying clean wasn't an option. "Careful," she warned as he came close. "Let's see if we can get him loose together."

They tried to free the terrified calf as the mother made anxious noises. Its little body was as slippery as a greased pig. As the calf thrashed in fright, finding a handhold was nearly impossible. It swung its head around and butted Leah's nose, making her eyes water. She lost her grip, sitting down hard in the cold mud and then getting back up with a groan. As she did so, she caught a glimpse of a grin before John managed to wipe it away.

"You okay?" he asked, straight-faced. His boots and gloves were already smeared with the noxious filth.

When she nodded, he pointed at her. "You've got mud on your cheek."

She could feel it, as well as the cold dampness seeping through the denim on her behind. "That's not the only place. Guess we'll have to tow him out. I'll be right back." As she struggled onto the wet grass, she slipped again, soiling both knees. Finally she made it over to Jewel, who waited patiently, and tied one end of her rope to the saddle horn. With no little effort, she and John managed to get the other end around the calf, who was bawling in earnest now. Despite the chill in the air and her heavy clothing, Leah could feel the perspiration trickling between her breasts and under her arms.

John's face—at least the parts that weren't streaked and smeared with mud—was flushed by the exertion of wrestling with the calf. His hat fell off, landing with a splat. "You're making it worse," he scolded the calf, wiping the Stetson on his pant leg before he plopped it back on his head.

Leah explained to John how she wanted him to

guide the calf, and then she walked Jewel slowly away from the bog. The rope became taut and the cow bellowed again. Duke barked, but Leah ignored him as she watched John and the calf.

"Okay," he shouted as the calf came loose of the bog like a cork from a bottle and slid on its back to firmer ground. After a stunned moment, it ran to its mother, who nuzzled it anxiously and then began cleaning it with her long pink tongue.

Waiting for the calf to begin nursing, Leah heard a muffled shout. She redirected her attention just in time to see John go down in the mud, face first.

She couldn't help herself. A whoop of laughter escaped before she could clap her hand over her mouth. With an expression of disgust, John levered himself back up. The sight of him made her laugh harder as she pulled a towel and her canteen from her gear. Something broke loose inside her, a combination of relief that the calf appeared to be okay and the giddy reaction to John's comic expression of mingled dismay and wounded male pride.

Leah doubled over helplessly as he got to his feet and advanced on her. Too late she realized his intention. Dropping the towel and the canteen to the grass, she tried to dodge him, but he scooped her into his arms and turned back toward the bog.

"No," she gasped, still laughing, "we'll get stuck. Put me down."

For a moment, she didn't think he would. Then, with obvious reluctance, he set her back on her feet.

Leah retrieved the canteen and wet the towel. As she stood holding out the scrap of fabric, John walked slowly around her in a circle. He began to chuckle.

"You're filthy," he said. "I hope you've got more towels."

Leah glanced down at the one in her hand and then back at him. The mud was already beginning to dry, hardening and cracking around the edges. He looked as though he'd been dipped in chocolate. She smiled.

John shook his head. She giggled. Finally, he threw back his head and roared with laughter. For several moments, they hung their heads, hands braced on dirty knees, and howled like two hyenas as the cattle, the horses and Duke looked on with benign puzzlement. Winding down, Leah took the towel and managed to wipe most of the mud from his face. Gazing at her intently, he did the same.

When they were done, the air seemed to crackle between them. John's gaze drifted to her lips. Involuntarily, Leah parted them slightly as she stood trapped by his stare.

His head dipped and then he caught himself. Abruptly he blinked and straightened. The moment shattered, Leah took a stumbling step backward.

"Even with a dirty face, you're pretty," he said in a low, rough voice.

Stunned, she could only stare helplessly. She was covered with mud and he thought she was *pretty?*

"You're crazy," she exclaimed gruffly when she'd found her voice.

His grin was fleeting. "If I'm crazy, then I guess you can't hold this against me." Lowering his head slowly, giving her time to protest, he pressed his cool lips against hers in a gentle kiss.

Chapter Four

John hadn't known he was going to kiss her until he did, and for just a millisecond, her mouth yielded under his. As her lips softened and heated, a groan worked its way up his throat. She pressed her hands to his chest and he lifted his arms to wrap them around her. Then her body stiffened in his embrace and she pushed against him.

"No," she murmured.

Heeding her halfhearted protest, John dropped his arms and let her go. Her eyes were wide, her cheeks flushed. Her mouth—dear heaven—her mouth looked sweet enough to devour in one more long, wet, drugging kiss. Unable to resist, he tipped his head again.

"Uh, this isn't a good idea," Leah said breathlessly.

He frowned. It seemed like a great idea to him.

Leah glanced around, and reason smacked him like a blow from a two-by-four as he realized how vulnerable she must feel. Except for Duke, who had taken off after some wild critter, they were alone in the center of the endless prairie. Had he frightened her?

"I'm sorry," John said quickly, raising a hand and then letting it fall back to his side when she flinched. "I didn't mean to make you uncomfortable." Slowly he backed away, giving her space.

"I—" Was that regret shadowing her eyes? He would have given a great deal to know what she was thinking as she searched his face.

She nibbled her lip. "It's okay," she said finally. More color ran up her cheeks. "I mean, it's not *okay*, but it just happened, right? Let's forget the whole thing."

"Good idea." Part of John was grateful she hadn't fired him on the spot, part of him was still trying to deal with his reaction to her. Damn, but she had a taste as sweet as cotton candy.

And he had absolutely no right to touch her, not when he didn't know whether he was committed to someone else. The realization was like a blast of ice water.

Somehow, he vowed silently, he'd sort through this mess and come out whole on the other side.

"Okay, then." She grabbed the canteen that had been dangling from her arm and sloshed more water onto the muddy towel, hands shaking. "Let's get cleaned up the best we can and eat lunch. There's a nice spot on the other side of those cottonwoods. Then I think we'd better head in and do something about these clothes." Glancing down at herself, she wrinkled her nose. "Ugh."

"At least we both smell the same," he observed with a forced grin. If she wanted to pretend the kiss had never happened, let her try. He could no more forget it than...he could forget his own name? His smile faded. Perhaps she was right. Silently he mounted Candy, the dried mud flaking off his jeans like dandruff, and followed Leah to the stand of cottonwoods.

Leah reined in and dismounted. "We're here. The trees will give us a little protection from the wind. In the summer the shade here is like an oasis from the heat."

She watered her horse in the stream and John did the same. When they were through, she busied herself with the saddlebags as Duke came bounding over to join them. As he drank noisily, she handed John half of the lunch he'd packed and a can of soda. Sitting cross-legged on the grass, she peeled off her gloves and dug a bag of dog biscuits from her pocket. She dumped them on the grass as Duke flopped down beside her, muzzle dripping. He devoured the biscuits and Leah took a hearty bite of her sandwich.

John was too hungry for more than an occasional comment as they ate. Leah's color was still high and she refused to look at him for more than a second at a time. With each bite, he did his best to put what had happened earlier out of his mind. Funny, he'd been struggling so hard to remember anything at all, and now he was trying to forget one of the few memories he had. Life was just full of little ironies.

Later as they rode along the fence line, Leah searched for breaks and damaged posts. If John's remote expression was any indication, he'd all but forgotten she was with him. The only sounds besides those the horses made were the faint sigh of the wind and an occasional harsh cry from a crow overhead.

Despite the discomfort of her damp, stiff jeans, Leah couldn't ignore the very real pleasure she was taking in being outdoors instead of cooped up in the library back in Caulder Springs. The sun had come out, gentling the wind. The carpet of grass at their feet was dotted with wildflowers—yellow peas, blue flax, orange wallflowers and purple vetch. Her grandpa had taught her their names. Soon the bluebells would be in bloom. It was days like this that reminded her why and how much she had always loved this land.

"What are you grinning about?" John asked, interrupting her thoughts.

Leah looked around again before answering. Did he think she was reliving that kiss? "I used to ride out here with my grampa," she said, so he would know she hadn't been thinking about him. "He was the one who bought this land years ago."

"Was he your paternal grandfather?" John asked. The mud on his hat had dried, giving it a two-toned appearance. The front of his jacket was caked with it. Leah would have to do laundry tonight so he'd have something warm to wear in the morning.

"My mother's father," she replied. "Daddy's family was down in Texas somewhere. He was a bronc rider before he was a rodeo clown. Grampa was the one who ran the ranch until he died." Her father hadn't been around much when Leah was small; he was always off rodeoing, even though the money he made never seemed to stretch past his next entry fees.

She could remember the excitement when he'd come home with gifts for Leah and her mother, followed later by the arguments when they thought Leah was asleep. Arguments about money and his drinking, and other things she hadn't understood.

"Grampa taught me to ride," she said to change the direction of her thoughts. "He got me a pony when I was three."

"You loved him a lot," John guessed.

She nodded. "I loved my daddy, too, but he was gone so much when I was young. He was a hero, larger than life." She wasn't sure why she needed to defend him. She'd always stuck up for him. He used to tell her she was the only one who understood. It made her feel special.

"And your mother?" John probed as they stopped for Leah to open a gate.

"What about her?" Leah asked after she had straightened back up. Her hands tightened on the reins. After her father's death, neither the ranch nor her only child had been enough to hold her mother's interest.

"You don't talk about her," he said mildly when he'd ridden through the open gate and was waiting for her to close it. "Is she still alive?"

Leah nodded. "She's staying in town."

"Why doesn't she live here with you? Did she get tired of the ranch?" He looked at the empty panorama surrounding them. "This could be a lonely life, especially for a woman."

Leah bristled at his words. "What right do you have to say that?" she demanded. "A lot of women run ranches. Mama worked hard for years and she's earned her rest." They were the same words Leah had told herself over and over. Mama hadn't rejected her, she'd just gotten tired. Leah didn't believe them and she doubted that John would, either. Somehow he would be able to tell that she'd been lacking as a daughter.

Leah slammed the gate shut and jerked on Jewel's reins, still fuming. Instantly she felt guilty and leaned down to pat her mount's neck in silent apology. "I'm the one who made the arrangements for Mama to live in town, so don't blame her for quitting," she told John.

"No one said anything about quitting and I'm not blaming anyone," he replied gently as they rode on. "But it sounds as though you do."

The comment caught her off guard. "Who said I blamed anyone? After Daddy died, it just got too hard for her, that's all. There were too many reminders. She's better off where she is."

"Does she live alone?" he asked as they reached a rocky patch. The trail was only wide enough to ride single file, so Leah moved ahead of him.

"Mama lives with two women, sisters, both widowed now," she replied when the trail widened and they were once again riding abreast. "They look after her." She wondered why she was telling him so much. Probably because he was a good listener. He appeared genuinely interested.

"Is she in poor health?" he asked.

"Not exactly." How could she explain her mother's condition? Depression sounded so inconsequential if you didn't have any experience with it. To avoid answering any more questions, Leah dismounted and examined a fence post that was leaning slightly. It showed no sign of rot or breakage, so she got back on Jewel and urged her forward.

Apparently John took the hint, or maybe he was just tired of the subject, because he didn't ask any more questions as the outbuildings finally appeared on the horizon.

Talk about Leah's mother made John feel restless, but he had no idea why. Although he tried, he couldn't remember his own mother. He tried to picture her face, to hear the sound of her voice, to recall one incident that she had been a part of—all to no avail. No matter how many times he'd failed to dredge up a memory since Leah found him, the disappointment was just as keen as it had been in the beginning. What kind of a son was he that he could forget the very existence of the woman who'd given him life? Wasn't it enough that he couldn't remember any woman he'd loved, any child he might have fathered, anyone else who mattered to him at all?

It wasn't until later after a long, restless night back in the tack room that something finally came to him, and then it wasn't a memory, it was a dream. A nightmare.

A woman was dying. John was sitting beside her, holding her hand. The light was dim, the room around them was in shadows, and he could hardly make out her face. Her voice, when she spoke, was faint, as though she was growing weak. He could smell her perfume, something flowery and familiar, and in the background was music he didn't recognize but somehow knew was her favorite. Only her hand, tightly gripping his, seemed real.

"Promise me," she said in a soft voice lined with steel. "Promise me you'll do this."

When he didn't answer, nearly choking on the sorrow that clogged his throat, she squeezed his hand and her voice rose. "I'll come back and haunt you if you don't."

The humor in her tone did him in. Part of him remembered her gentle laugh, even though he couldn't picture her face. His eyes filled with tears and he was nearly overcome with a deep, chilling sadness.

"Promise me," she said again.

Before he could ask her what she wanted, the image started to fade and darkness filled the room.

"No," he exclaimed, gripping her hand tighter. "Don't go. Tell me who you are and what you want me to do."

"Promise me." It was just a whisper.

Suddenly the room was full of light. He blinked against the brightness and realized that his hand gripped only a fistful of the coarse blanket that covered him. He was sitting up in bed.

As his eyes focused, he saw Leah standing in the doorway, her hands tightly clasped together, her expression anxious.

"You were having a bad dream," she said. "I'm sorry that I woke you, but you were shouting, and I could hear you all the way up at the house. I thought maybe your head was bothering you."

John followed the direction of her gaze and looked down at his plain white T-shirt. He raked a hand through his hair, struggling to get his bearings and to remember the snatches of dream, which were already fading.

"I'm okay," he said. "Thanks."

She backed out of the doorway. "I brought your

jacket." She pointed to the chest by the door. The parka was no longer covered with dried mud and beside it sat a steaming mug of coffee. "I'll give you a few minutes."

"I'll be right out," he replied as she shut the door behind her. Perhaps a dose of caffeine would sweep the cobwebs from his brain. Pulling on his clothes, he tried again to hold on to the bits of the strange dream that floated in his head like brightly colored scraps of paper, but all he could remember was a woman's voice. *Promise me,* she kept pleading.

When he came out of the tack room a couple of minutes later, Leah was turning out the horses at the other end of the barn. She glanced at him and looked away without speaking. If he'd been shouting in his sleep, she probably thought he was nuts. He wondered if she'd heard what he was saying, but he was almost afraid to ask.

By the time he'd splashed water on his face in the tiny bathroom and come back out, sucking down the coffee as if it were plasma and he a vampire, she'd gone outside.

John looked around and found her bent over Jewel with a hoof pick. The morning before he hadn't known the names of the tools she'd lined up along the top rail of the corral fence. Today he remembered them easily, rasp, currycomb, sweat scraper. Somewhere inside him was the knowledge to use them. Did that mean his memory was returning?

Biting the bullet, he went over and asked if she'd been able to understand anything he was shouting.

"Just the word *mother*," she replied as she straightened and arched her back to get the kinks out. "The rest was pretty garbled."

Shocked, he watched her pick up another hoof.

"I'll be right back." He felt guilty for not pitching in right away, but part of him needed to be alone— to take in what she'd told him. The woman he'd known in his dream to be on her deathbed, the woman whose face had been no more familiar to him than a stranger's, was his mother.

It was the first real glimpse of his past that he'd had, and he *hated* it. Feeling shaky, John went back into the barn. Except for a cat that melted into the shadows, it was quiet and cool. There he sank down onto a hay bale and buried his face in his hands.

Vaguely, he was aware of Leah's approaching footsteps, but he couldn't summon the will to lift his head and pretend things were normal. Not this time.

"Headache?" she asked, bending over him and touching his shoulder. "There's aspirin in the tackroom cabinet." When he looked up, her gaze slid to the gash on his forehead and then back to his eyes. He'd forgone the bandage last night; the wound was scabbed over. It was going to leave a scar she had solemnly assured him would be "chick bait."

He wanted to wrap his arms around her waist and hide his face in her feminine softness. The impulse shocked him. How weak a man was he?

"No, I'm fine." He tried for a reassuring smile. A little of the anxiety faded from her expressive face, but she appeared to be in more of a hurry than the day before. Then he remembered that she'd told him she had to work at the library this morning. They'd discussed what he could do, clean stalls again, help with the feed and then go through a list of repairs she'd written down for him. By the time he'd done all that she'd be home again.

John got to his feet, intent on pulling his weight. Leah stepped back, but when she looked up at him, her gaze was still intent, seeking. It made him nervous.

"Is your mother still alive?" she asked gently.

"Sure," he replied without thinking. "She has a condo in Florida and she's hooked on bingo."

"That sounds like a good life." She glanced at the plain watch on her wrist and frowned. "I'll go fix breakfast and then I have to change for work. You know what to do?"

He patted the pocket where he'd put her list of instructions. "Got it all right here."

"The number for the library is up at the house, on the pad by the phone." She nibbled on her lip. "Miss MacPherson frowns on personal calls at work, but if you really need to talk to me—"

"I understand. I won't bother you unless the barn catches fire."

Her eyes widened.

"Bad joke. Sorry." He put a hand on her shoulder

and gave her a gentle shove. "Get going. I'll cope."
What he needed was time alone and some mindless
chores, a chance to think and maybe sort things out.

"Give me a few minutes to get breakfast on the
table and then come on up," she said, walking backward toward the door as she talked. Today she was
wearing a red shirt beneath her jacket, and its brightness gave color to her cheeks. Her hair swung
straight and silky around her face. "I'll fix you a
couple sandwiches while I'm throwing together my
lunch." Duke followed after her, tail wagging. He'd
hardly glanced at John this morning. The dog must
have decided he wasn't much of a threat.

"Great. I'll get to work," he said as she hesitated
in the doorway.

"Candy's waiting for you. The tools are still outside."

Just as Leah had said, the gray horse was waiting
patiently by the fence, cross-tied between it and a
post. When he saw John, he pricked up his ears. After John had cleaned the animal's hooves, he ran
back into the barn and retrieved his coffee mug. Then
he went up to the house, ignoring the little spurt of
eagerness he felt.

After they'd eaten a much simpler breakfast than
the day before, he went back to the barn, carrying
the sack lunch and the soda she'd handed him before
she headed upstairs to get ready for work. When he
heard the truck start up, he thought about stepping
outside to wave, but he didn't. For the next several

hours, he kept his hands busy while his mind replayed his mother's message.

Promise her what? He had no idea.

Leah spent the morning shelving books, a job she especially detested and one that took up at least an hour every day she worked. Today it took longer because two classes from the grade school came in. Miss MacPherson was in her office looking through new book catalogs, so Leah hurried over to the main desk when the line of children began forming in front of it to check out their selections. The librarian never looked up from her reading.

Right before Leah's lunch hour, Amy Stout, the janitor, came in. She and Leah got along well, in part because of their mutual dislike of Miss MacPherson. Amy and her husband lived in a small house at the other end of town. He had opened an insurance agency the year before and her job at the library was part-time. Her stomach was beginning to round out beneath her flowered uniform smock and Leah envied her with a pang that was bittersweet.

"How you feeling today?" Leah asked.

Amy had been suffering from morning sickness for several months, but she refused to quit her job despite her husband's urging. She had confided to Leah that her paycheck went right into a college fund for baby Stout.

At Leah's question, she made a face and waved at Miss MacPherson, who had glanced up from her reading and was watching them through the glass wall of her office. Technically, Leah was on lunch and Amy didn't start for another fifteen minutes. She usually came in a little early so they could visit before she went to work.

"My stomach wasn't actually as queasy this morning," Amy said. "Maybe the doctor was telling the truth after all when he said it wouldn't last forever." She followed Leah into the tiny employee lounge and shut the door behind them. If any patrons came in, Miss MacPherson would just have to deal with them.

"What's new?" Amy asked as Leah retrieved her lunch from the ancient refrigerator and they sat down at the scarred wooden table. No doubt she expected Leah to reply as she always did. Not much.

"I hired a temporary ranch hand," she said with a small grin at Amy's double take. She hadn't intended to say anything; the words just popped out on their own accord.

"Really? Is he cute?" Despite her pregnancy, or perhaps because of it, Amy had stepped up her insistence that what Leah needed most in her life was a man. She knew all about Gil, Leah's ex-husband, but Amy didn't consider one failure a reason to remain alone. There weren't that many single men in town, but both Amy and Carter, her husband, were constantly offering to fix Leah up with anyone who had the misfortune of crossing their matchmaking paths.

"Yeah, I guess he's attractive," Leah replied

slowly. If Amy ever found out that John had kissed her, she'd have no peace.

"You guess?" Amy echoed, leaning closer. "Haven't you noticed? Where did you find him?"

"On the side of the road." Leah took a big bite of her sandwich and chewed slowly while Amy's eyes widened.

"A hitchhiker?" she exclaimed. "You actually picked up a hitchhiker? Don't you know how dangerous that can be?" Amy was from Detroit. In a lot of ways, she was still adjusting to rural Colorado.

While Amy waited, impatience dancing in her brown eyes, Leah swallowed the bite of sandwich and washed it down with a sip of cola. Amy gazed at the soda can longingly. She'd given up caffeine for the length of her pregnancy.

"Well, are you going to tell me?" she demanded finally. "I have to go to work in a couple of minutes, you know."

"He was lying in the grass at the foot of my road," Leah said, pausing for effect. "He was unconscious."

Amy popped up out of her chair. "Ohmygod! Are you serious?" she squealed. "What happened to him?"

"I'm not sure. He says he was hitchhiking and he had a disagreement with the man who picked him up. He said he must have fallen and hit his head." Even to her own ears, put that way, John's story sounded as lame as a three-legged dog.

"What did Sheriff Brody think of him?" Amy asked.

Leah ducked her head and rooted around in her lunch sack for the carrot sticks she'd brought. "The sheriff hasn't exactly met John."

"John?"

"John Brown."

"Did he have references?" Amy demanded, hand on her hip. "Did you check them out?"

Leah bit into a carrot and shook her head, wishing she'd never mentioned John at all. "He's only staying for a few days."

"How many days does it take to murder you and dispose of your body?" Amy cocked her head, pursing her lips.

"I was desperate," Leah said defensively. "Wranglers who will work for room and board aren't exactly thick on the ground. Ever since Eli left, I've had more work than I can do alone." Amy thought she was crazy to try to run the ranch by herself. She just didn't understand how important it was to Leah.

Now her friend looked distinctly skeptical. "Maybe Carter and I should come out and look him over," she offered dubiously. "Carter could have a little talk with him."

Leah had to suppress a smile. Carter was tall and skinny, with glasses and thinning hair. The idea of him putting the fear of God into anyone was ludicrous to everybody but Amy, who idolized him. "Thanks," Leah said, touched by the suggestion.

She wouldn't hurt her friend's feelings for the world. "But I did ask the sheriff if any ax murderers were on the loose in the area and he reassured me there weren't."

There was a frown on Amy's round face. "But what do you really know about this guy?"

Before Leah could answer, Miss MacPherson poked her head into the lounge. "Amy, would you clean the rest rooms first thing?" she asked in a not-too-subtle reminder that it was time to start work. "After the school visit this morning, I'm sure they need attention."

With her back to the librarian, Amy rolled her eyes at Leah, who had to struggle not to react. "Will do," she said as she followed the older woman to the door. "I'll talk to you later," Amy told Leah pointedly.

Had there been a hint of warning in that last remark? As Leah dug a paperback mystery out of her purse and settled down to read for the rest of her lunch break, she was sure she hadn't heard the last from Amy on the subject of her new employee.

As it turned out, Amy left work early that afternoon with a migraine headache, so the subject didn't come up again. On her way home, Leah picked up a pizza and placed the box on the seat beside her. She slowed when she drove past the spot where she'd found John two days before.

She was looking forward to getting home, she realized, even more so than usual. Was it because of him? She had to remember that he was only going to be around for a few days. He felt as though he owed her, and any help he gave her was that much less she had to do herself.

That's all there was to it. Just because he'd kissed her didn't imply anything more. She was a grown woman, not a naive schoolgirl, and she recognized a pass when she saw one.

She loved the ranch and her animals, especially the horses, and she was eager to get home to see them. That was all.

When she pulled up in the yard and John walked out of the barn, wiping his hands on a rag, she ignored the surge of excitement she felt at the sight of him.

"How was your day?" he asked as he came over and opened her door before she had the chance.

"It was nothing special," she replied, grabbing the pizza box and hopping down to the ground. "How did things go here?" Good grief. They sounded like a couple chatting away about their day.

"Well, I didn't burn the barn down," he replied. "Wow, pizza!" he exclaimed when he saw what she was holding. "It smells heavenly."

"I thought it would be quick and easy," she said somewhat defensively. If he expected a home-cooked meal every night, he could forget it!

Instead, he reached into his pocket. "What do I owe you?"

Leah turned away. "Room and board, remember?

That was the agreement. You're not paying for part of this pizza.''

He tucked his money back into his pocket and took the box out of her hands. ''Are you angry about something?'' he asked as Leah headed for the house.

She turned back to him impatiently. ''Of course not. I'm just tired and hungry, that's all. And I can't wait to get out of these clothes.''

John studied her full cotton skirt and plain white blouse with a thoroughness that made her squirm. ''They look nice enough,'' he concluded, ''but they aren't the real you.''

How did he picture her? Jeans and boots? ''And what's the real me?'' she demanded. He didn't know her at all.

''Something soft,'' he mused, walking around her in a slow circle. ''Feminine. I think there's a secret side to you that likes satin and lace. Girlie things.''

His reply stunned her. Made her feel vulnerable. In defense, her chin went up. ''Not very practical,'' she drawled.

He leaned closer, balancing the pizza box like a serving tray. ''I think you have an impractical side,'' he whispered.

Leah's gaze drifted to his mouth, so close she could lean forward and—

She blinked. ''Pizza's getting cold,'' she said.

Was that disappointment that flickered in his eyes, quickly doused? His grin was easy, revealing nothing.

"Sure. Let's eat." It was her turn to scamper after him.

"How'd you do on the list I left?" she asked as she followed him up the porch steps.

He stood aside and let her go in the house first. "Okay. I got everything on your list done except for replacing that post. I couldn't find anything to use, so we'll have to buy something, I think."

She wondered if he realized he'd said "we" and not "you." "Everything else on the list?" she exclaimed. She'd never dreamed he'd get that much done. She'd just figured working down the list would keep him busy.

He nodded, a grin slashing his face.

A few minutes later, when she had reheated the pizza in the oven and they were sitting at the table, she remembered what he had said earlier and mentioned his mother again. "You must miss her." Florida was so far away.

A shadow crossed his face and his expression turned grim. To her utter confusion, his mouth tightened.

"It was probably for the best," he said. "She'd been ill for a while and she hated being dependent on anyone."

Chapter Five

"Are you telling me now that your mother is dead?" Leah demanded.

John glanced down at the piece of pizza he'd been about to bite into. His face registered acute dismay. He set the pizza back down without answering, and Leah tried to remember exactly what he'd told her earlier that day. She was sure he'd said his mother lived in a condo in Florida—and that she liked bingo. What was going on?

"It's complicated," he said now.

"Complicated?" she echoed. "Either the woman is alive or she isn't." Her own mother's situation leaped to mind, but she dismissed it. Quality of life wasn't the issue here.

"It's not what you think," John protested, but he didn't meet her gaze.

Leah sat back and folded her arms across her chest, a sinking feeling in her stomach. "You don't know what I'm thinking."

For several long moments, she waited to hear his explanation. The only sound in the room was the ticking of the old grandfather clock in the corner. John had lied, but why? And what else had he lied to her about?

Amy was right. Leah didn't know anything about him and she'd been a fool to trust him. Even now as he sat and watched her, he was probably trying to decide what new story would work best with her.

And she had *kissed* him!

Cautiously, Leah slid back her chair and got to her feet. "I'll be right back." To her own ears, her voice sounded brittle. The phone, right there in the living room, was out of the question. So was the rifle she kept in the coat closet. Her father's pistol was in the top drawer of her nightstand. Perhaps she could get to it before John's suspicions were aroused. She tried to smile, but her cheeks felt stiff.

"Leah, wait," he said quietly. "There's something I need to tell you." When she hesitated, he said, "Please. Sit down, would you? Give me a chance to explain."

She glanced around at the heavy vase by the couch, the fireplace poker, even the butter knife on the table, looking for potential weapons. Duke was somewhere outside. If she ran, would John grab her? Would he erupt into some kind of monster? Perhaps it was better to pretend to go along with him.

Never taking her gaze from his, Leah sank back down into her chair and waited expectantly. She gripped the edge of the table, knuckles white, to keep her hands from trembling.

Absently John began picking pepperoni slices from the nearly forgotten pizza sitting between them and stacking them in little piles. Leah eyed the door and wondered if she should run for it.

"I have amnesia," he said baldly.

"What?" She stared, struggling to make sense out of what he'd just said. "Amnesia?" she repeated dumbly. "You mean you've lost your *memory?*"

"That's right." A flush darkened his cheeks, as though it were something to be ashamed of.

Leah sat back in her chair and expelled a long breath. Good golly. "Why didn't you tell me this before?" she asked, puzzled. Several things she'd thought odd now slid into place. His reluctance to talk about himself. His hesitant manner and his vague answers to the questions she'd asked. What a nightmare for him.

It was John's turn to look confused. "I could be anybody," he said. "A bank robber. A murderer. An escapee from a mental hospital. I have no idea."

No. Just hearing him reel off the possibilities and seeing the torment in his eyes was reassurance to Leah that he was probably none of the above. For a timeless moment, she searched his face, and then she came to a sudden decision. "Let's find out," she said briskly, getting to her feet once more and heading for the phone. She wanted to believe him, but she had to be sure.

"Wait!" There was panic in his voice. "What are you going to do?"

"Call Sheriff Brody," she replied, one hand on the telephone receiver. "He's probably still in his office and he must have access to a list of missing persons. Can you remember anything? Where you're from?"

He shook his head, but at least he wasn't trying to stop her from calling.

"What about your duffel bag?" she asked. "Were there any clues in it?" As he shrugged, a sudden thought occurred to her. "Is John Brown your real name?"

He held up his hand. "The only thing I found was this. My ring is inscribed to J.B. Probably a coincidence." For a moment, he looked so achingly vulnerable, so alone that she was tempted to go over and put her arms around him. She couldn't imagine what it would be like to lose your entire identity.

Then realization hit with a sickening thud, sticking her feet to the floor. He could be married, with a family. Oh Lord, how that idea hurt.

Leah felt selfish for even considering her own feelings right now. Some poor woman somewhere could be worried sick about him. He might have children who were going to bed at night wondering where their daddy was.

She remembered the way she had returned his kiss, had thought of kissing him again and fantasized about more, and she burned with guilt.

"You need to know who you are," she insisted, picking up the receiver. *She* needed to know, too. Before she was able to dial the number, John came over and covered her hand with his bigger one.

"What if I'm wanted by the law?" he asked, voice hoarse. "What if I'm some kind of fugitive?"

She studied him carefully. "I don't believe that for a moment."

He shook his head. "You can't know."

"My instincts are usually pretty good," she insisted. "But what if you have a family somewhere worrying about you? A woman who loves you and who's wondering where you are, why you haven't called her?" It hurt to say out loud, but the possibility had to be faced.

"I don't think so." He thumped his chest with his fist. "Somewhere in here, I'd *know* if I loved someone."

John swallowed thickly. He'd almost said "someone else." But he didn't love Leah. It was too soon. He was just attracted to her sweetness, her energy and the way she had of smiling as though she were reaching out to him alone.

She wasn't smiling now and she didn't appear to be buying his reasoning. "Let's call the sheriff and see what he can find out," she suggested without taking her hand from the receiver. "Okay?"

At least she wasn't waving a butcher knife at him and insisting he clear out. Sensing this was some kind of test, John stepped back, hands spread wide. "Yeah, go ahead. I guess you don't have any choice but to turn me in."

"That's not what I'm doing," she protested. She leaned forward and laid a hand to his cheek. "It will be okay." Her voice was husky. Then she turned away and dialed while he waited, his guts twisting into a knot of dread.

"I can't find anything to indicate who you might be," Sheriff Brody told John as the three of them sat in the cluttered office in Caulder Springs. He was younger than John had imagined, with dark brown hair and a mustache. "No one matching your description has been reported missing or wanted for anything that I can see." As he talked, he set aside a stack of forms.

Leah looked disappointed. Part of John was relieved.

"The other thing I can do is to take your fingerprints and see if they're on file anywhere, but that will take a while."

John stiffened and set down his coffee cup. One taste had convinced him all law enforcement officers must have lead-lined stomachs. "You mean find out if I have a criminal record?'' Not everyone was as trusting as Leah.

"There are a lot of different reasons," the sheriff replied calmly. "They would tell if you've been in the military, for example, or held some kinds of government jobs. It would be a start."

"It's voluntary?" John asked.

Sheriff Brody's eyes narrowed slightly, but his reassuring smile didn't waver as he sat back in his chair. "At this point." In other words, until or unless his suspicions were aroused for some reason.

An intense feeling of claustrophobia washed over John and he got to his feet. He wasn't ready to deal with this, he realized.

Leah looked up at him. "What are you doing?" she asked.

"Thanks for your time," John told Sheriff Brody. He looked at Leah. "It doesn't sound like I'm a serial killer," he said. "Let's go."

Her eyes widened. "Aren't you going to let the sheriff find out what he can?"

She didn't understand. The feeling of panic grew stronger. "The sheriff has been a big help." He glanced at the other man, then back at Leah. "My memory will come back on its own," he insisted. "We can give it a few days, can't we?" He wanted to plead with her for time, but he was loath to do it in front of the other man, who was watching them both with a professional interest John could almost feel.

Leah switched her attention to the sheriff, who shrugged his khaki-clad shoulders. "He's right. From what I know about amnesia, his memory could come back all at once, with no warning, or a little at a time in a series of flashbacks." He made a notation on his pad. "Have you had any of those?" he asked John.

"So far it hasn't been anything that definite," he admitted, remembering the woman in the dream. "It's more like strong feelings, vague impressions, that's all."

"Can you give me any examples?" the sheriff asked.

"Like being pretty sure I'm not married," John told him without looking at Leah. "I don't know why. I just feel that way."

The sheriff studied him without comment. It was an effective interrogation technique, John realized. It made him want to spill his guts in an attempt to convince the other man he was telling the truth. With a sheer effort of will, he stayed silent and returned the sheriff's gaze with one he hoped didn't look too shifty-eyed.

Finally the other man sat forward, his chair squeaking in protest. Although his office was cluttered with cartons, files, papers, various pieces of equipment and used disposable cups, his desktop was nearly bare. There were no pictures or personal objects, just more papers, neatly stacked, a brass desk set that looked rather incongruous there and a coffee mug full of pens. A black phone sat next to a tattered

Rolodex. Behind him on the wall were framed certificates that John couldn't make out and last year's calendar. It was turned to December, with a photo of a German shepherd wearing a Santa hat.

Now Sheriff Brody closed the manila folder he'd opened at the start of their interview and tapped it with his finger. John wondered what his notes contained. Just the facts, few as they were, or his observations, as well?

"Will he be staying with you?" the sheriff asked Leah.

She glanced at John, whose gut tightened as he held his breath.

"Yes," she said after a barely noticeable pause. "He's doing chores around the ranch for me."

"How are you managing out there?" the sheriff asked her. "I heard Eli quit."

"That's right. He moved to St. Louis to be with his daughter. John's been a tremendous help."

"Taylor Buchanan was in the other day," the sheriff said quietly as he scratched his sideburn. "Asked if I'd seen you lately."

Leah stiffened in her chair, her sudden tension communicating itself to John. Who was Taylor Buchanan? A boyfriend? She hadn't mentioned anyone. From the tightening of her mouth, it was more likely he was a rejected suitor.

"What did you tell him?" she demanded.

"Nothing."

"Good." Her tone was grim. "That's how much

about me is any of that man's business. If he's hoping to get his hands on more of my land, he'll have to whistle for it.''

The sheriff rose, bringing the interview to a close. "Didn't you used to baby-sit for the Buchanans?" he asked.

Leah's chin jutted out as she got to her feet. "That was a long time ago. I was a teenager. Unfortunately, people change and not always for the better.''

"There are some who'd say Taylor was just doing his duty when he turned in your father," the sheriff replied in a neutral tone.

Leah pressed her lips together, but she didn't say anything more. John wondered if she would tell him about the situation if he asked. The sheriff's comments had aroused his curiosity.

"Nice to meet you," he told John with a penetrating stare as he stuck out his hand.

"Thanks for your time." John shook it firmly.

"Let me know if you want me to do anything more," the sheriff replied easily. "There are avenues we can pursue if you don't start to remember things on your own."

John nodded and glanced at Leah. Even being here voluntarily made him nervous and he was anxious to leave so he could ask her more about this Buchanan fellow. "Ready?"

She still looked annoyed. "Yes." She thanked the sheriff for seeing them, but the earlier warmth had gone out of her voice.

"So tell me," John said as soon as they were outside on their way back to Leah's pickup. "Who is this Taylor Buchanan and what did he do to you?"

"Killed my father," she said shortly, "stole part of my land and ruined my life. Isn't that enough?"

As John stopped in the middle of the wooden sidewalk and gaped at her, Leah felt a little ashamed for exaggerating, but not much. Taylor Buchanan had been instrumental in bringing on the events leading to her father's death, and even though he'd paid a fair price for the land, she would never have sold it in the first place if her father had lived. Nor would her mother be where she was now.

Tossing her head, Leah climbed behind the wheel of her truck and looked expectantly at John. "You coming?" She was shocked that he hadn't wanted to do everything possible to find out who he was. How could he stand not knowing?

Also, she was still annoyed that Buchanan had been asking about her. Why couldn't the man leave her alone to get on with her life the best she could? Since her father's death, Taylor had offered to lend her money, had sent over a couple of his men to help with the roundup and had made her a standing offer to buy more of her land. He also came by periodically to check on her.

If he was trying to make up for what he'd done to help tear her family apart, he could jolly well give up. She didn't trust his intentions and she would never forgive him.

John sat down next to her in the cab of the truck and turned to study her profile. Defiantly, Leah started the engine and switched on the radio, cranking up the music loud enough to discourage conversation. From the corner of her eye, she saw John drumming the fingers of one hand on his knee. Ignoring him, she pulled out of the parking spot and headed for home.

Finally John reached over and turned the radio down.

"What do you think you're doing?" Leah demanded, knowing she was acting like a brat but unable to stop herself.

"If Buchanan did everything you say, why isn't he in jail?"

She glared at John. "He's a wealthy rancher. He and his brother, Donovan, were big-time rodeo stars. Unlike my family, the Buchanans have influence around these parts."

"I don't think any of that would cut much ice with Brody if they committed a crime." John's tone was dry.

Leah's hands tightened on the wheel. "I told you my father was a bullfighter. Do you know what that is?"

John nodded. "That's the rodeo clown who keeps the bulls away from the riders after the buzzer goes off."

"Or if they get hurt, or hung up in the rigging, it's the clown's job to help them," she elaborated. "The work's a lot more difficult than it looks. Unlike most broncs, bulls don't stop just because the clock does. They're vicious and unpredictable. And they're surprisingly quick for their size.''

"Sounds pretty dangerous," John commented. "Your father must have been a brave man."

"He risked his life every time he went into the arena and he prevented a lot of riders from getting hurt," she agreed. "But then a rider was killed in the ring and they blamed my dad."

"That's awful. What happened?" John asked.

She pushed the hair back off her forehead. "It was an accident. The rider was thrown and the bull got between him and Daddy. The other clown was standing in the barrel, waving his arms and trying to distract the bull, but it turned the wrong way. The rider was still down and the bull gored him. There was nothing anyone could do." She took a deep breath. "Afterward, they said Daddy was out of position, that his reactions were slow and he wasn't aggressive enough."

"What did Buchanan have to do with it?" John asked.

"He was there. It was his testimony that got Daddy fired. Word got around. After that, none of the other shows would hire him."

"I'm sorry." Briefly, John rested his hand on her leg. "What did your father do after that?"

"He stayed home and ran the ranch. Mama liked having him around all the time, but I don't think his heart was in it. He drank too much, and they quarreled a lot. Then I went away to school, and while I was gone he got killed. That's when I came home to stay.''

For a few moments there was silence in the cab of the truck. ''And later on Buchanan was the one to buy up some of your land?''

Leah nodded. ''We share a common border and he's always wanted to get his hands on it.''

''Sounds as though he had a vested interest in testifying against your father,'' John said in a grim voice.

''Now you know why I don't want anything to do with the Buchanans.''

''Some people don't care who they have to hurt to get what they want.'' John spoke like a man who'd had some doings with people like that himself.

Leah would have liked to ask him about it, but she suspected he probably wouldn't be able to answer and the question would only frustrate him. Instead, she turned off the main road and pressed down on the accelerator. It was late and the animals still needed tending. She was lucky to have John to help her with the chores, but she also wanted some time to sort through her feelings about him and what she'd found out today.

Was he telling the truth about his memory loss? She had no reason to think otherwise, but his unwillingness to try to find out his identity still rankled. How could she allow herself even the slightest feelings of attraction toward a man she knew nothing about, not even his real name?

Later that night, John lay on his cot in the tack room wondering the same thing. How could he stay here, attracted to Leah the way he was, when he had no idea what he'd left behind or what waited for him to return? Somewhere out there he must have a life, a job, a place to live. Possessions, a pet, friends. Parents, family? He shied away from the idea that he might have children, an ex-wife. So why was he reluctant to let Sheriff Brody try to find out who he was?

John shifted restlessly on the narrow bed and punched his pillow before he jammed it back under his head. As he stared into the darkness, listening to the night sounds the horses made in their stalls, an image of a woman popped into his head. A pretty woman with dark hair.

Bits of an argument floated through his mind. No, not an argument exactly. There was sadness, but no anger. The woman was crying as she folded clothes and put them in a cardboard carton sitting on a bed. John was watching her, torn by mingled relief and regret.

He tried hard to remember more, what they'd said, who she was. As he narrowed his eyes and peered into the darkness, searching for clues, more images faded in and out. Scenes of the two of them laughing, talking, walking together. Waking up next to her. It all felt so distant, so long ago, but he couldn't tell if that was because of the amnesia. There'd been some kind of break between them, though, he was sure of it.

Finally, exhausted, he gave up with only a vague idea who the woman was and what she'd meant to him.

As he lay in the darkness, sleep eluding him, he tried hard to remember other things in his life. Maddeningly, the answers seemed to linger at the edges of his consciousness, just beyond his grasp. It was as if his mind could deal with only so much at a time and no more. With a frustrated sigh, he finally gave up. His head was beginning to throb dully. Glancing at the luminous dial on his watch, he turned over, squeezed his eyes shut and willed sleep to come.

The next morning when Leah came out to the barn, John was already up and dressed. When she handed him a steaming mug of coffee, he barely grunted his thanks. He looked tired.

"Didn't you sleep well?" she asked as he turned away, pitchfork in hand. It was barely dawn, but he'd already turned out several of the horses, including the two with foals at their sides.

"I'm okay." His tone discouraged further questions.

Leah watched him walk away, his shoulders slightly bent as though the weight of the world rested on them. Making a sudden decision, she hurried after him.

"Are you sure you don't remember anything about where you're from?" she asked. She'd been thinking about it half the night, trying to find a way to learn more about him. When she got to the library, she was going to call the sheriff and ask if there was anything he could do without John's consent. Even if *he* didn't have to know, she did.

John swung back around, eyes blazing. When she saw his expression, Leah stumbled to a halt. He held the pitchfork in one hand, the coffee mug in the other.

"Damn it, Lisa!" he exclaimed. "Leave me alone."

Leah's whole body stiffened. "Who's Lisa?" she asked.

John shook his head. "Leah. I meant to say Leah."

"No," she responded quietly, heart aching. "You said Lisa, plain as day. It was no mistake. You've remembered something, *someone,* haven't you?" She swallowed past the lump in her throat and took a deep, steadying breath. "John, is Lisa your wife? Is that what you've remembered?"

Chapter Six

"No, Lisa wasn't my wife." John was sure of that, as certain as he was of standing here now, but how to convince Leah? He leaned the pitchfork against a post and walked outside, his head starting to pound with the effort of sorting out the hazy images that darted through his brain like minnows and then disappeared before he could analyze them.

Hands on hips, he frowned at the ground. A light rain had fallen during the night, just enough to dampen the dust in the yard and leave it clinging to his boots. The air had a sharp, metallic scent to it. At least the sky wasn't a leaden gray, the ground beneath him a stew of deep, gluey mud and puddles of standing water like—

"Is your memory starting to come back?" Leah asked, excitement in her voice as she darted around him and peered into his face.

Refusing temptation, John shook his head regretfully. "Not really. I mean, I get flashes, but that's all." For a moment he let himself believe that her interest was personal, that she might even feel a twinge of jealousy toward Lisa. Then common sense prevailed. He and Leah barely knew each other. It should be enough that she'd taken him in and not thrown him out when she realized everything he'd told her about himself was a fabrication.

"So you think you aren't married, but you don't really know?" she asked casually, leaning over to pat the orange cat he'd seen hanging around the barn.

John's heart gave a little jerk. Was it possible she did care whether or not he was free? That she returned some of the sizzling attraction he felt toward her? She'd given no indication, other than not slapping the hell out of him when he kissed her.

She was holding the cat she called Sassy as she watched him with an expression of mild curiosity, nothing more. Purring, the cat butted her chin and Leah scratched behind its ears. Duke was nowhere around. He was probably out chasing rabbits—an exercise in futility, according to Leah.

"I do know I'm not married," John insisted, trying to think of some way to convince her. Tugging off his glove, he held up his bare left hand. "I don't wear a wedding band," he said triumphantly.

"There's no mark on my finger to indicate that I ever did."

"Lots of men don't wear rings," she countered. "My ex sure didn't. That doesn't prove anything."

There was a bitter edge to her voice that John had never heard before. "I didn't know you'd been married," he exclaimed, taken by surprise.

"It's nothing I brag about," she replied dryly. "I've been divorced for over a year." Her tone made it clear the subject wasn't open to discussion. While John did his best to squash his curiosity, Sassy began to squirm in Leah's arms, so she set the animal down with a murmured endearment and a last loving stroke.

Watching her hand on the cat's fur, John imagined her touch on his bare skin. Fire raced along his nerve endings, distracting him from their discussion, and he realized he was grinning foolishly.

"I have work to do," Leah said, expression haughty.

Before she could go back into the barn, he reached out and grabbed her arm. The very air seemed to crackle between them.

"Don't run away just yet," he coaxed.

She stopped in her tracks and looked pointedly at his hand, but he didn't release her. He was curious about her marriage and why it had ended, but he could tell now wasn't the time to quiz her.

"I remembered Lisa leaving me," he said instead.

"I know she meant something to me at one time, but we definitely broke up. I'm sure of that."

Leah relaxed slightly, but her eyes were troubled. "Maybe your memory is starting to come back, or perhaps it's just what you want to think."

"Why do you say that?" he asked, genuinely puzzled.

"So you won't have to deal with the idea of anyone worrying about you while you refuse to even try to find out who you are."

Frustrated, John let go of her arm. "Why do you care?"

Leah's cheeks went pink. "Why don't you?" she countered, stepping away from him. "It's unnatural not to want to have an identity. What are you scared of, anyway?"

Scared? He wasn't afraid of anything and he almost told her so. And then that sense of nagging dread returned. And the pleading voice. *Promise me.* But what had he promised? And why did he not want to remember?

Leah was still waiting for a reply.

Determined to prove his point, John captured her hand in his. When she didn't protest, he tugged lightly until she was standing very close. Her eyes widened with surprise and her lips parted.

"I know the kind of man I am," he growled. "If I was married to someone else, I wouldn't be doing this." Then he gave in to the temptation that had been eating at him since she'd first sashayed into the barn. Dipping his head, he covered her mouth with his.

He'd meant to take out his frustration in a punishing kiss, but as soon as his lips touched hers and he felt the slow heat rising between them, his brain shut down and pure sensation took over. For a timeless moment, she responded, kissing him back, her hands clutching his shoulders. Then, just as desire threatened to completely overrun his self-control, she broke away and pressed her hand to her mouth.

"Don't do that again!" she exclaimed, eyes blazing. "Married men kiss other women all the time. That doesn't prove anything. Until you're willing to find out who you are, you have no right to touch me."

"Maybe other men act badly, but I'm not one of them," he argued. "I may not know much about myself, but I do know that."

Clearly unconvinced, Leah whirled around and stalked back to the barn. Her back was rigid with disapproval, her hands curled into fists at her sides. The cat ran after her, meowing hopefully.

She was one stubborn woman. She exasperated him. For some reason John didn't want to look at too closely, Leah's opinion mattered a great deal. He hated for her to think of him as a cheat or a coward, but he didn't know what to say that would satisfy her. There were still way too many things he didn't understand himself.

* * *

"Thanks for letting me know about this," Leah told the sheriff in an undertone. "Keep me posted, okay?" Looking over her shoulder to see where the librarian was lurking, Leah said goodbye and set the receiver back down. Despite Miss MacPherson's disapproval of personal phone calls, Leah had wanted to ask Sheriff Brody if there was anything he could do to find out John's identity without his consent. To her surprise, the sheriff admitted that he'd already sent in the prints he'd lifted from John's coffee mug. Now all they had to do was wait for the results.

"Have you boxed up the discards for the book sale yet?" Miss MacPherson asked from behind her as she stood nibbling on her lip. "The volunteers want to start setting up the table sometime tomorrow."

Wondering how much, if any, of her conversation with the sheriff Miss MacPherson had overheard, Leah took a deep breath and swung around. To her relief, the older woman's face revealed nothing but vague annoyance, her habitual expression.

"I'll get right to it," Leah promised. Every so often, the collection had to be culled, the outdated books discarded to make room for new ones. Going through the shelves with a list of titles to be pulled was dusty, boring work, but today Leah welcomed it. She needed to keep her mind off the problem of her employee and his identity. Sheriff Brody might not have filled in any of the blanks surrounding her mysterious drifter yet, but John's prints could prove something. Leah just hoped that the news, when it came, wasn't bad.

"What's wrong?" Miss MacPherson was staring at her suspiciously.

"Nothing at all." Leah kept her expression as neutral as she could and headed toward the science section with her list as two elderly women came in the front door. With a smile and an effusive greeting that grated on Leah's ears, Miss MacPherson hurried over.

No doubt the fact that both women were regular patrons and Gertrude Lawrence's husband served on the board of trustees had something to do with the librarian's attitude. Tuning out their chatter, Leah glanced at the clock. Amy would be in shortly, probably full of questions for which Leah had no answers. Until then, she had work to do.

Later that day, John was in the barn cleaning tack when he heard a truck pull up outside. Leah had come home twenty minutes before, but she'd gone directly into the house. John figured he'd give her another half hour before he went looking for her. Although he'd been mulling over their earlier conversation all day, he still had no idea what to say to her. What he did want to tell her was that while he was at the house fixing himself lunch, an image of some kind of office had come to him, along with the feeling that he belonged there. Despite how much he enjoyed working at the ranch, his regular job might involve sitting behind a desk.

Although he had visualized a computer, ledgers, file folders and rolls of what might have been blueprints in the office in his mind, trying to picture himself as an accountant or a draftsman of some kind had gotten him nowhere. All he had for his trouble was a slight headache.

Now he was curious who their visitor might be. Leah hadn't said anything to him about any riding lessons being scheduled after work today. Before he could show himself, the screen door slammed open and her footsteps clattered forcefully down the porch steps.

"What the hell are you doing on my property, Buchanan?" she shouted.

Hearing the open hostility in her tone and recalling what she'd told him about the other man, John decided to stay out of sight for the moment in case there was trouble. Let Buchanan think Leah was alone and make some move or even threaten her. John would be on him like a rabid dog.

Carefully, he peeked around the open doorway of the barn. Shock hit him like a bucket of melted snow when he saw that Leah was standing in front of the house with her feet spread apart and a rifle nestled in the crook of her arm.

He should have known she could take care of herself, he acknowledged with a wry shake of his head.

She'd been doing just that since way before he'd come along.

A late-model pickup with a loaded gun rack was parked in the yard. A tall man wearing the standard ranching uniform of boots and jeans paired with a handsome brown suede jacket was standing with his back to John. His hands were hooked in his belt, and despite Leah's hostility, he appeared to be totally relaxed.

"Ashley and I just wondered how you've been," he said, stopping a few feet away from her. "Did the roundup go okay?"

John could hear every word easily and he could see Leah's angry expression. If she was scared, she didn't show it. Muscles tensed, he wondered if he should duck back inside and grab the pitchfork, just in case.

"You've got a lot of nerve coming on my land," Leah replied in a hard voice to her visitor's query. "And this *is* still my land." Her face was flushed with temper and her nose was stuck in the air. "How I'm doing is none of your business, so there's no point in your sniffing around here."

John felt a bubble of pride at her tenacity. According to Leah, this man was her sworn enemy and a powerful member of the local community, but she was facing him down without a visible qualm.

"We've known you for a long time, Leah," Buchanan replied in a conversational tone, as if there were no bad blood between them. "We worry about you." He was sure as hell arrogant.

She shifted the rifle warningly. "Don't you bother your head about it. I can take care of myself. Thanks to your meddling, I've had no choice these last few years."

John thought he saw the other man flinch, but he wasn't sure. What did he want, anyway? He sure had a hell of a nerve, coming here as though he had some right to poke into her business.

"I know you blame me for a lot of things, but Ashley and I still care a great deal about your welfare," Buchanan said. "A pair of coyotes have been spotted over east. Larson says they got two of his calves the other night. Have you had any trouble?"

"No, I haven't. *My* calves are all nice and healthy." Leah pressed her lips together and stared Buchanan down.

"We heard you hired a drifter no one seems to know much about," he continued, obviously unperturbed by her rudeness. "Just wanted to make sure you're okay."

"Who I hire or what I do is none of your business," she replied coldly. "Your ilk isn't welcome here." For emphasis, she waved the gun, although she didn't actually point it at him. "You don't own all my land, so you can just get off what's still mine right now."

"Okay, Leah, have it your way. Just promise

you'll let me know if you need anything, won't you?''

In the face of her open animosity, he sure didn't give up easily, John thought with a shred of grudging respect. The man must have one hell of a guilty conscience eating at him.

''I'd sooner call on one of those coyotes to guard my calves,'' Leah stated. ''Are you going to leave on your own or do I have to call the sheriff?''

''The sheriff is well aware of the truth of the situation between us and you know it,'' the man replied, making John wonder what he meant. The truth about what? Buchanan's railroading her father and buying part of her land when she was desperate for money?

''I'll let you be for now,'' Buchanan continued. ''Sooner or later you'll have to listen to reason. When you're ready, you know where I am.''

His words sounded like a threat to John, who would have liked nothing better than to run him off personally. Instinct told him Leah was too intent on sticking up for herself to welcome a champion at this point, though. Grimly, he stayed where he was.

She remained stubbornly silent, her eyes narrowed with dislike. Twin patches of color highlighted her cheeks. The rifle was clutched in her hands so tight that her knuckles showed white.

Caught up in the image of glorious womanhood she presented, John nearly forgot to duck out of sight as the other man shrugged, swung around and walked back to his truck. As he did, John caught a glimpse of his face below the brim of his hat.

For a moment, the impression that he'd seen Buchanan somewhere before perplexed him. He stared hard but, as usual, he couldn't remember. Stopping only to touch his fingers politely to his hat brim, a gesture Leah refused to acknowledge, Buchanan climbed back in his truck, started the engine and drove in a slow half circle out of the yard. As he did so, John noticed a logo on the driver's door.

Buchanan Brothers Enterprises was written in gold script framed by a painted lasso.

Pretty fancy, John thought with a sneer.

"What are you doing here, spying on me?" Leah demanded. While he'd been watching Buchanan's retreat, she'd marched over and was looking up at him with the light of battle still glowing hotly in her clear blue eyes.

John glanced down at the rifle and then back into her face. If she hadn't been armed, he might have been tempted to taste her sweet mouth again, but he wasn't a fool. She'd probably turn on him like a bad-tempered badger.

"Gonna shoot me?" he asked instead.

Obviously surprised, she glanced down at the gun as if she'd forgotten she was even carrying it.

"Oh heck, it's not even loaded," she taunted. "Don't be scared."

It was the second time his bravery had been called into question, and it was enough to shatter his resolve. This time when he reached for her, though, she met him halfway.

Tossing aside her good sense along with the gun, Leah launched herself at John like a groupie at a rock star. Her breasts flattened against his chest and her mouth pressed into his, her adrenaline running like molten lava as she opened to him, tasting, stroking, greedy for more of the passion that flowed from him in waves. He groaned deep in his throat as she wriggled closer yet. His hands clamped on her waist and he backed her against the wall. His thigh nudged its way between her legs, nestling into her heat.

With a little moan of surrender, she stretched up to bury her hands in the hair at his nape and managed to knock his hat askew. Her breasts throbbed and her nipples tingled as the feelings tumbled over one another inside her—desire, frustration, hunger, excitement and a nameless craving she couldn't begin to identify.

John lifted his mouth fractionally and she moaned. Her fingers tightened on his scalp, seeking to anchor him close as she brought his mouth back to hers. She kept her eyes squeezed shut and he responded by kissing her more deeply than before. Leah's senses spun dizzily.

His hold on her shifted and the world tilted at a crazy angle as he scooped her into his arms. Reluctantly, she peeked at her surroundings. He was carrying her into the dim recesses of the barn. Only when he shouldered his way into the tack room and lowered her to the cot he'd been using did she begin to come to her senses.

"What—what are you doing?" she stammered.

His eyes smoldered with desire and she wondered for an instant if it was already too late. Had she pushed him too far or would he stop if she asked him to?

"What do you want me to do?" he demanded hoarsely. His face was flushed with passion, his features drawn tight with it as his gaze cut to her mouth. Before he could lower his head again and draw her back into the mindless whirlpool of passion that threatened to engulf them, she shook her head and pressed her hand to his chest.

"We can't," she gasped, every nerve in her body crying out for her to sink back with him into the maelstrom. "We don't know if you're married or not."

His face darkened and she wasn't sure if it was anger or frustrated desire that stained his skin. "*I* know," he replied. He dropped his arms and straightened, leaving her huddled on the blankets. "Either you believe me or not. Which is it to be?"

For a timeless moment, Leah stared up at him, struggling to accept what he said and knowing, deep inside, that *he* believed it. Finally she bowed her head. The risk was too great. Taking him into her body and her heart, as well, then finding out his instincts had been wrong and he *did* belong to another woman would exact a bigger price than she could afford to pay. It could very well break her heart.

"I'm sorry," she said, scrambling to her feet in the quiet stall. "It's not that I don't think you're telling the truth—"

Before she could finish, he held up a detaining hand. "No, don't apologize," he said roughly. "It's me who should be sorry. Dragging you in here the way I did and insisting that you believe me." He turned away from her, head hanging. "Hell, you don't know me that well. I don't even know myself."

It was Leah's turn to silence him. She put a hand on his arm and felt his muscles shiver beneath her touch. "Don't beat yourself up over this," she told him, striving for lightness. "I haven't fired you yet, have I?"

His gaze, when he looked at her, was hooded. "Perhaps you should."

His warning tone sent a trickle of nervousness through her. "Why?" she asked. "Have you remembered something else? Are you a man on the run, after all?"

"Damned if I know any more," he replied grimly.

"Maybe supper will restore you," she suggested. "I've got stew in the Crock-Pot and sourdough bread in the freezer. Are you hungry?"

He looked at her and then his gaze shifted to the pile of blankets in the corner. "Hungry doesn't even begin to describe it," he said dryly.

Ignoring her own leaping response to his comment, Leah ducked around him and stepped into the wide aisleway. "Let's eat now and then finish the chores afterward," she suggested. She needed to get out of here. Without looking to see whether John was following her or not, she headed for the house. Before she could take more than two steps, his voice stopped her in her tracks.

"If you and Taylor Buchanan are such enemies, why did he come by today?" he demanded, closing the gap between them. "Does he have the hots for you, too?"

Leah's reaction to the jealousy in John's tone was mixed. As she faced him, her chin jerked upward defiantly.

"I already told you that I have no use for the man," she said. "When I was a kid I'd baby-sit for him and his wife. The one good thing I will say about him is that as far as I know, he's never looked at another woman since they came here. He adores Ashley. When I was at their house, he never treated me in any manner that made me uncomfortable." She remembered the arrogant way he'd stood there and asked how she was doing, as if the gun she were holding didn't exist. "He's probably just keeping an eye on the rest of the land he hopes to acquire someday. He must be getting impatient. I'm sure that's why he asked how the roundup went."

She and John started walking together toward the house. "He looked familiar," John said. "Not that I could remember if I'd met him, of course."

Leah glanced up at him. She hadn't thought about it, but the two men resembled each other in a general way, especially dressed as similarly as they were. "Look in the mirror," she said flippantly. "With your cheekbones, the cleft in your chin and your matching Stetsons, you and Buchanan could probably be brothers."

John hesitated, frowning, and then he stared off into space as if he were no longer with her. His thick brows were bunched in concentration and there was a tightness at the corners of his mouth.

"Are you okay?" Leah asked nervously after he had remained silent for a good half minute.

He blinked and then his gaze refocused on her. "Huh?"

"I asked if you were all right?" she repeated, relief trickling back slowly. "For a moment, you kind of went somewhere else."

To her surprise, he grabbed her upper arms and a wide grin splashed across his face. "I think it's coming back!" he exclaimed. "My memory. By bits and pieces, it's starting to return."

Happiness for him washed over her, followed almost immediately by a sense of foreboding. Would the return of his memory take him away from the ranch, from her? She liked having him around and not just because he helped with the chores.

"What is it you've remembered?" she asked, holding her breath. Was it something more about his not being married? Something specific?

"After you said that Buchanan and I could be brothers, I remembered very clearly that I was an only child. It wasn't one of those crazy flashes I've been getting. I saw myself with my mother. She raised me alone, I'm sure of it."

He sounded so elated that she was loath to push him. He hadn't mentioned a father, and there was so much further he had to go. Hoping for John's sake that he was right about the veil of amnesia lifting, she slapped a smile on her face and gave him a quick, impersonal hug. "That's wonderful," she said, stepping back before he could react. Perhaps soon they'd both have some answers.

Chapter Seven

"I have tomorrow off and I need to run to town for supplies," Leah told John over supper a couple of days later. "Do you want to go with me?" There was always a chance someone he knew would recognize him, but that wasn't going to happen if he stayed at the ranch. He hadn't mentioned any more returning memories and she hadn't asked. "We could grab a bite at the café if you want, maybe catch a movie," she added.

John's brows rose and his hazel eyes crinkled at the corners as he grinned. "Are you asking me out? Because if you are, I accept."

His smile scrambled Leah's senses. Looking at his mouth reminded her of the kisses they'd shared. Unsure just how to deal with his teasing tone, she took a bite of her chicken leg. As she chewed, she tried to think of some flip, clever comment and failed utterly. When he smiled at her the way he was doing now, it was hard enough to breathe normally, let alone be witty.

"In fact," John continued as he forked up more green beans, "I'll take you to dinner. Is there a decent restaurant in Caulder Springs? Besides the pizza parlor?"

"Well, there's the Blue Dog, but you don't have to make a big deal out of this." He must have been able to tell how much he'd flustered her, and now he was gloating. Irritation crept into her voice. "I'm tired of my own cooking, that's all. I haven't visited Mama since before you showed up, so I need to stop by and see her, too." Leah pushed the mashed potatoes around on her plate. "Since you apparently don't have any means of transportation other than your thumb, I just thought you'd like a ride to town."

As soon as the last nasty comment was out of her mouth, she longed to call it back. John had done nothing to deserve it except make her feel attractive, even desirable for a moment.

He stared at her while she struggled not to fidget, appalled by her own rudeness. She couldn't speak. Then he helped himself to a biscuit, spreading honey as carefully as if it were gold leaf. A pink flush swept over his face from his jaw to his chiseled cheekbones.

"Sorry, boss, I didn't mean to overstep my bounds," he said in a tone devoid of expression. "I'd appreciate the lift, if you don't mind. I need to pick up some underwear and another pair of jeans, if there's a place that sells clothes. What time did you want to leave?"

Dang it. Now she'd gone and hurt his feelings. The last thing Leah wanted to deal with was how long it had been since she'd found herself in a social situation with a man. Not since Gil left her, she realized now.

Obviously her manners were more than a tad rusty. Exasperated, she blew out a breath and rocked her chair onto its back legs. How to make amends without adding to the sudden strain between them?

"Compton's probably sells everything you need, unless you want designer jeans or those silk boxer shorts the yuppies wear. I figured on leaving by two, after chores."

"I wear briefs, and plain white will do fine. I'll be ready when you are." His tone was flat, but strain snapped between them like river ice breaking up.

"What about a compromise?" she suggested cautiously. "You buy dinner and I'll pay for the show."

He tipped his head to the side assessingly. "If we were dating, that would be called dutch treat."

Leah breathed a sigh of relief as the tension eased a notch. "We're not dating."

"Then I get to pick the movie," he replied straight-faced.

PLAY "LUCKY 7" AND GET
THREE FREE GIFTS!

HOW TO PLAY:

1. With a coin, carefully scratch off the silver box at the right. Then check the claim chart see what we have for you — **FREE BOOKS** and a gift — **ALL YOURS! ALL FREE!**

2. Send back this card and you'll receive brand-new Silhouette Special Edition® novel These books have a cover price of $4.25 each in the U.S. and $4.75 each in Canada, b they are yours to keep absolutely free.

3. There's no catch. You're und no obligation to buy anything. W charge nothing — ZERO — f your first shipment. And you don have to make any minimum numb of purchases — not even one!

4. The fact is thousands of readers enjoy receiving books by mail from the Silhouet Reader Service™ months before they're available in stores. They like the convenience home delivery and they love our discount prices!

5. We hope that after receiving your free books you'll want to remain a subscriber. Bu the choice is yours — to continue or cancel, any time at all! So why not take us up on ou invitation, with no risk of any kind. You'll be glad you did!

YOURS FREE!

PLAY LUCKY 7 FOR THIS EXCITING FREE GIFT!

THIS SURPRISE MYSTERY GIFT COULD BE YOURS FREE WHEN YOU PLAY

LUCKY 7!

The Silhouette Reader Service™ — Here's how it works:

Accepting your 2 free books and mystery gift places you under no obligation to buy anything. You may keep the books and gift and return the shipping statement marked "cancel." If you do not cancel, about a month later we'll send you 6 additional novels and bill you just $3.57 each in the U.S., or $3.96 each in Canada, plus 25¢ delivery per book and applicable taxes if any.* That's the complete price and — compared to the cover price of $4.25 in the U.S. and $4.75 in Canada — it's quite a bargain! You may cancel at any time, but if you choose to continue, every month we'll send you 6 more books, which you may either purchase at the discount price or return to us and cancel your subscription.

*Terms and prices subject to change without notice. Sales tax applicable in N.Y. Canadian residents will be charged applicable provincial taxes and GST.

If offer card is missing write to: Silhouette Reader Service, 3010 Walden Ave., P.O. Box 1867, Buffalo, NY 14240-1867

BUSINESS REPLY MAIL
FIRST-CLASS MAIL   PERMIT NO. 717   BUFFALO, NY

POSTAGE WILL BE PAID BY ADDRESSEE

SILHOUETTE READER SERVICE
3010 WALDEN AVE
PO BOX 1867
BUFFALO NY 14240-9952

NO POSTAGE
NECESSARY
IF MAILED
IN THE
UNITED STATES

"Deal." She took a drink of milk and then she grinned. "In case you *forgot,*" she teased, "there's only one movie house in Caulder Springs and it's not a multiplex. More like third run."

He narrowed his eyes suspiciously. "What's playing? Not some girlie thing, I hope, all drippy and romantic."

"I have no idea. What kind of movies do you like?" she asked curiously. "Big guns, lots of explosions and car chases, fake blood?"

He thought for a moment and then he shrugged. "Danged if I can remember," he drawled.

For some reason, his reply struck Leah as hilarious. She tried to stop the laughter, pressing a hand to her mouth, but it just sputtered out between her fingers. Helpless with it, she turned sideways in her chair and doubled over as her eyes filled with tears.

After a moment, John chimed in, his hearty chuckles a counterpoint to her burst of laughter. Duke, lying down across the unlit fireplace hearth, pricked up his ears and looked at the two of them as though they'd lost their minds. One of the cats that had sneaked in unnoticed jumped down off the couch and padded over to meow at the door. Still giggling, Leah dabbed at her streaming eyes and got up to let it out.

"What kind of movies do *you* like?" John asked when she sat back down, gasping for breath and grinning like a fool. The laughter had loosened something inside her, reminded her that life wasn't always a dark ride.

She thought for a moment. "I don't like to be scared," she said. "I hate gore and flailing body parts, but I want a good story."

He just looked at her. "Flailing body parts?"

"I like Mel Gibson and Tom Cruise." She sighed. "George Clooney, Nicholas Cage."

John rolled his eyes.

"Do you remember any of them?"

"Yeah." He ran a hand through his hair. "It's just the personal stuff that eludes me."

For a few moments they resumed eating in silence. "Why does your mom live in town?" he asked after he'd cleaned his plate, wiping up the gravy with the last bite of biscuit. "Doesn't she like the ranch? You never really said."

Leah poked at her beans with her fork. She ate vegetables because they were good for her, but she didn't care for them. Talking about her mother usually made her feel uncomfortable, inadequate. Raised questions for which she had no answers, like what she could have done differently to pull Mama back from the brink.

"It started after Daddy died," she said without looking up. Meticulously, she dissected a bean into three pieces with her fork. "She just started to fade, as if she were withdrawing from life. I thought it was the grief and I left her to work it out for herself. Then one day I asked her to run an errand for me to the vet's office in town. I didn't have the time and Gil, my husband, wasn't around. She started to cry, big silent tears." That day still haunted Leah, and she could picture the panic on her mother's face. "That was when I finally realized she didn't go outside the house anymore. She hadn't set foot off the ranch in weeks, maybe since the funeral, and I hadn't noticed," she added bitterly. "I was too busy."

"Well, who was running things around here?" John demanded. "Did you have a foreman, a manager?"

She gave him a look of disbelief. "Are you kidding? Does this look like the King Ranch? Daddy ran it with two wranglers. After he died, one of them refused to take orders from a woman and quit."

He quirked an eyebrow. "The woman being you?"

"That's right." She'd been dealing with the stock, the books and the bills—a lot of bills—as well as her own crumbling marriage. "One day I came in from the range and saw that the house was dirty, the dishes weren't done and we'd run out of groceries. Mama had stopped getting dressed, but I thought it was temporary. Then she stopped getting out of bed."

"It sounds as though you had a lot on your plate," John remarked. "Your husband, did he help?"

Leah remembered how Gil had complained that she didn't have enough time for him. He'd been one more problem when what she desperately needed was solutions. "No," she said starkly. "Except for tearing apart the machinery, Gil didn't much like ranch work.''

John made a sound of disgust and shook his head. ''Maybe you're being too hard on yourself.''

''He was good with cars,'' Leah explained, rising to Gil's defense just as she always had with her folks, even in her own mind. Maybe it was her choice of husband she was really defending. ''He could take an engine apart and put it back together with his eyes shut. After Daddy died, Gil wanted me to talk Mama into selling the ranch so he could open a garage in town. We argued about it.'' She made a helpless gesture. ''This was Mama's home, the only one she'd ever had. How could I do that?'' Even though her mother had stopped caring about the ranch, Leah had hoped at the time that her feelings might change.

Gil had been impatient. Before Leah ever saw the problem coming, he and his boss's wife at the gas station where he worked part-time ran off together. Hank Abbott had been livid. He'd hired a private detective. Leah had done her best to ignore the whispers, the questions, but she hadn't contested the divorce Gil wanted. Her pride was in tatters by then, along with any feeling she'd had toward him.

''What happened?'' John asked gently. He'd propped his elbows on the table, resting his chin in one hand and giving her his undivided attention. His hazel eyes were like warm honey.

''He left town and we got divorced,'' she said shortly, unwilling to admit the death of her marriage had been one more thing she just hadn't noticed. "End of story."

John's eyes narrowed, but he didn't probe any further. "And your mother?" he prompted instead.

"When she refused to get out of bed, I realized we needed help. I couldn't manage the ranch, the house and her meals, too. Doc Hershaw said there was nothing wrong with her physically. He prescribed some pills. She didn't take them. He recommended counseling. She refused."

John sat back in his chair. "Was there no one else to help you?"

"No one I felt comfortable asking. Mama was an only child, like me, and Daddy's family was scattered." Not one of them had come to his funeral. She remembered her panic and the crushing sense of failure when she'd realized her mother was slipping away from her no less surely than her father had.

"The winter was a bitter one and we lost some cattle." She swallowed hard as visions of that bleak time filled her mind, the unrelenting cold and the snow, day after day. Struggling to keep the truck on the slippery roads as she and Eli hauled feed to the cattle and broke through the crust of ice in the water troughs. Numbness in her fingers and needles when they thawed, eyes that reddened, watered and stung, wind that cut through the layers of clothing like a jagged knife. Just thinking about it, she shivered and hugged herself.

"When spring came, there were losses. I had no

choice but to sell off some land to Buchanan.'' If she'd done that before Gil left, would he have stuck around? Would she have cared? They were questions without answers. ''I'd hired a neighbor's wife part-time. She tended Mama while her kids were in school, but after a while that wasn't enough. Doc Hershaw found the two women who agreed to take her in. They're widows and they appear to enjoy fussing after her. She seems content and they don't charge too much.''

''Does your mother go out?'' John asked. ''Does she ever come here?''

Leah frowned. ''Oh, no. She hardly ever leaves the house, except maybe to sit in the garden. Irene and Rosemary love their flowers. I try to stop by every week or so, but I don't think time means much to Mama anymore.'' Leah pushed back her chair, wrung out from all the emotion she'd dredged up. ''She doesn't miss me or this place, at least.''

John watched her carry the dirty dishes to the sink, her forlorn voice still echoing in his ears. She'd been through enough to beat down anyone, let alone a slip of a thing like her, and yet it seemed only to have made her stronger.

''So why do you stay here?'' he asked. ''You could sell the ranch, start over somewhere with a tidy nest egg. Surely this Buchanan would buy you out.'' It seemed like a reasonable question.

She looked appalled. ''It's my *home*. Daddy would hate my selling, especially to Taylor Buchanan.'' She nearly spat out his name. Apparently she considered that answer enough. She didn't elaborate.

"Did Buchanan give you a fair price for the land he bought?" John asked. Perhaps the other man had taken advantage of her plight, set up her father with an agenda of his own in mind. Some things were awfully hard to prove, but there were moral laws as well as civil ones. This Buchanan had sounded reasonable enough when he was here, but that didn't mean he wasn't used to getting what he wanted.

Her expression turned cold as she glanced over her shoulder. "You don't understand. Buchanan waited, like a vulture, until I was forced to sell. No price was fair."

"What exactly happened when your father lost his job?" John asked, getting to his feet and helping to clear the table as Leah ran water in the sink. Over the past few days, they'd developed a routine of kitchen cleanup, moving easily around each other in the confined area.

"Don't you dare blame my father for any of it!" she cried, stopping so quick that John nearly plowed into her. "It was Buchanan who passed judgment on him, and Buchanan who benefited from it." She turned her back, but not before John saw her wipe at her eyes. He put his hands on her shoulders in a clumsy attempt at comfort, but she pulled away from his grasp.

"No one understood how dangerous Daddy's work was, or how much courage it took for him to go into the arena over and over again.'' She looked up at John, her eyes filled with tears, mouth trembling. ''He'd been gored once and nearly trampled. He was scared. Every time he got in there with the bulls, he had to wrestle with that fear and overcome it.'' She hiccuped and buried her face in her hands, shaking her head. ''No one else understood,'' she repeated, mumbling. ''But I did.''

Now she did let John comfort her, so he abandoned his questions. ''It's okay,'' he said awkwardly, patting her back as she cuddled against his chest. Her tears dampened his shirt. Standing there and hearing her pain, he felt useless and clumsy.

Finally she sniffed noisily and stepped away. He dug into his pocket and handed her a bandanna handkerchief.

''Thanks,'' she muttered, wiping her face with it.

What kind of man was Buchanan, John wondered, to take advantage of someone with a family? How did a person like him sleep at night? And what, exactly, had he done to get her father fired? Thrown his weight around, called in some markers? Maybe even greased a few palms?

Judging from how upset Leah was already, now wasn't the time to ask. Maybe, if he ever ran into the other man again, he'd ask him instead.

''Mama, this is my friend John Brown,'' Leah told the older woman sitting in the rocking chair with a quilt over her lap.

The resemblance to her daughter was easy to see, although Leah's mother appeared much older than John would have expected. Her eyes, a darker shade of blue than Leah's, darted to his face. A hesitant smile deepened the grooves bracketing her mouth. She raised a wrinkled hand to her short, curly gray hair, patting it nervously before she smoothed the collar of her housedress.

"Hello, Mrs. Randall," John said, leaning down.

She returned his greeting without any real interest in him. Her gaze didn't linger and he felt as though he'd been dismissed. Leah's neighbor had shown more curiosity about her new hired hand than her own mother did.

Leah perched on the edge of a chair and twirled a strand of her hair around her finger while John sat on a maroon velvet sofa that felt like padded concrete. Lace doilies were pinned to the arms and needlepoint pillows surrounded him. On the opposite wall was a glass cabinet full of antique dolls. A nearby piano was covered with framed photographs. A clock ticked loudly.

Rocking slowly in her chair as she stared through the lace window curtains, Leah's mother answered her questions, lapsing into contented silence between each one. She asked no questions of her own—not about the ranch and not about her only child. While Leah chattered about the weather, the flower garden, the new kitten she'd taken in, John watched the two of them and let his mind wander.

They'd stopped at a small clothing store first, jammed to bursting with racks of jackets, shirts and jeans for every member of the family. Shelves of boots and hats lined one wall. John bought underwear, jeans, socks and two new shirts while a tiny woman Leah introduced him to twittered around like a nervous bird.

Now he was looking forward to dinner and the movie. Funny, he could recall other shows he'd seen, but nothing about who he'd gone with or where he'd been at the time. Memories of the impersonal things in his life were coming back first and he wondered why.

He was trying to conjure up some image of where he lived or worked when he realized that Leah had gotten to her feet. She kissed her mother's lined cheek, so he bade the woman goodbye.

"Who's the young man?" Mrs. Randall asked, clearly startled, so Leah repeated her earlier introduction. After more goodbyes, John followed her from the room. Looking back, he saw that the older woman had turned her attention to the window.

"She's already forgotten we were here," Leah said softly.

Hearing the sadness in her voice, John squeezed her shoulder. "But you haven't," was all he could think of to say.

The two older women he'd met on the way in were seated at the kitchen table playing cards. One wore a flowered dress and a string of pearls at her neck, the other a pink sweat suit and tennis shoes.

"Is she eating?" Leah asked them.

"Like a bird," replied Rosemary, who was wearing the dress. "She likes her chocolate, though."

"I'll bring her some next time I visit," Leah promised. She opened her purse and took out a check.

"Thank you, dear." Rosemary folded it in two and stuck it in her pocket without looking at it.

"Call me if she needs anything," Leah said. "I'll see you next week."

"Bring your young man with you again." Irene, the other sister, winked at John. "We don't have many male visitors anymore."

Leah's face flamed and John chuckled. "I'll be back." He took the hand she thrust at him. It was thin, with blue veins, swollen knuckles and a diamond so big it looked like glass, so he was careful not to squeeze too hard. The feel of her brittle bones teased at his memory, but the half-formed impression was gone before he could grasp it.

"Take some cookies," Rosemary insisted, thrusting a covered plate at him. "Chocolate chip, fresh baked this morning."

Thanking her, he followed Leah down the back steps to her truck.

"I'm starved," she said as soon as they were both inside. The aroma from the cookies filled the cab. "How about you?"

"I could eat." He looked longingly at the covered plate sitting between them on the seat.

As Leah drove through town, she didn't mention her mother or their visit, so neither did he. Instead she identified the businesses they passed. None of them rang a bell with him, as if he'd dropped out of the sky onto her property. If it hadn't been for the local newspaper he'd found in her living room, he wouldn't even know what state he was in.

For all he could trust of what he knew, he could have lived here all his life. But then wouldn't someone recognize him?

As they passed the pizza place, the talk turned to food: Chinese, which they both liked; Thai, which Leah hadn't tried; and the Mexican they were headed for at the Blue Dog.

"The hotter the better," John said, surprising himself. Why couldn't he put a location to the restaurants he remembered: Frosty's, the Crab Cracker, Armadillo Barbecue, Clifford's? Leah didn't know any of them.

Since John didn't have a license, Leah was driving. "Want to stop by the sheriff's office?" she asked as they passed the station. "We have time. Perhaps he's heard something."

John gritted his teeth and tension curled in his gut. His head began to throb and he touched a hand to the scabbed-over gash on his forehead. "Not today."

Her mouth looked pinched as she turned her at-

tention back to the road. Clearly she didn't understand his reluctance. "Okay."

"I suppose you think I should talk to him," he
said, feeling defensive and pressured despite her
agreement. How could he explain? His attitude confused him, as well.

"It's your life." Her attention stayed on the road
ahead as she slowed for a dog that wandered in front
of the truck.

"That's right, it is." Suddenly John felt petty for
trying to stir up an argument. Seeing her mother had
to be difficult for Leah. Mothers were supposed to
be supportive, nurturing. Leah didn't need him picking at her, too.

"I'm looking forward to dinner," he said by way
of a silent apology.

Leah glanced over and gave him the sweet smile
that never failed to melt some of the ice around his
lonely heart. "Me, too." There was relief in her gaze
and more, as if she was looking forward to the evening together as much as he was.

She had dressed up for the outing, wearing snug
jeans in a soft shade of lavender and a purple, blue
and white striped shirt with a stand-up collar under
a light blue windbreaker that exactly matched her
eyes. There were small pearl studs in her ears and
she was wearing perfume, something light and flowery. He, of course, was wearing a pair of worn jeans
and a plaid shirt from his limited wardrobe. At least

he'd polished his boots and dusted off his borrowed hat.

John wished he'd thought to tell her how pretty she looked, but when she'd come downstairs he'd been unexpectedly tongue-tied. Had he really imagined her plain at first?

She glanced over, her gaze colliding with his before it slid away. The silence between them grew awkward.

"Uh, you look very nice," he stammered, wondering what the heck was wrong with him. Surely he could do better than that around an attractive woman. Had he been such a bumbling clod in his former life? He sure hated to think so.

"Mama likes me to dress up a little when I visit," she said as she slowed and turned the corner. "She'd rather see me in a skirt, but having to wear them to work is bad enough."

And he'd assumed she had fussed with her appearance for him. That should teach him to jump to conclusions. He didn't say another word until they pulled up in front of a stucco building painted an alarming shade of blue a little way outside of town.

Later, through their excellent Mexican dinner and during the movie that followed, John tried to read between the lines they exchanged and figure out what she was thinking. When he reached for her hand in the darkened theater, she didn't pull away but laced her fingers with his and held on tight as they both watched the screen. By the time the movie, a science fiction thriller about the battle of two worlds, was over, John had come to a decision.

"Let's get out of here," he said as the houselights came up. Ignoring the curious glances of the other patrons, he held tight to her hand as he urged her up the aisle.

Leah nodded to several people in passing, but she didn't stop to talk. When the two of them walked outside, darkness had fallen. By the time they got to the truck, parked behind the building, the small crowd from the theater had scattered in other directions. Before Leah could open her door, John reached past her and did it for her. When she turned her face to his, smiling in the golden glow of a nearby streetlight, he moved closer, spurred on by the attraction and need humming through him all evening. Their bodies were almost touching.

Leah's eyes, made luminous by the night, widened slightly and her lips parted. Perversely, testing them both, John stepped back.

"Let's go home," he said, holding her door. His voice sounded rough to his ears and his tongue felt sluggish. Despite the chill in the air, he was hot and more than a little edgy, on the brink of something he couldn't name.

Without speaking, Leah climbed in the truck and he shut her door. Her face was a pale oval as he circled around and got in beside her. She started the engine and turned on the radio. As if by mutual consent, the ride home was conducted in silence except for the steady stream of country music. John kept time with it by tapping his fingers on his knees while he did his best to ignore what was building between him and the woman beside him. When they finally pulled into the yard and she turned off the engine, the sudden silence wrapped around them like a living thing.

Leah turned to John and he swallowed thickly.

"I had a nice time," she murmured, as if they'd been on a date.

"So did I." They stared at each other.

"As soon as I change, I'll be out to help you with the animals," she said.

John's hands curled into fists. "I can manage if you're tired," he offered. "I know the routine."

"I'm sure you do." She seemed to be considering his offer. "When you're done, you could come to the house," she suggested. Her voice had altered, becoming uncertain. She licked her lips as if they were dry. "I've got some of dad's whiskey, if you'd like a drink."

John tried to decipher what she was really saying, but all he saw in her face was indecision. He would have liked to tell her not to invite a man in if she hadn't made up her mind about what she was offering. Instead, he nodded slowly and silently cursed himself for a fool. "I won't be too long."

They got out of the truck and Duke was waiting to greet Leah. After she praised him and stroked his head, he came around and accepted a pat from John, neither responding nor rejecting the touch. When she walked toward the house, John stood and watched her in the glow from the yard light. Right before she reached the steps, she turned, waving, and then continued on inside.

As soon as she disappeared through the door, John whirled and hurried toward the barn. He might not remember much, but he knew that nothing matched the feeling of having a woman you cared for in your arms, and he realized beyond a doubt that he cared for Leah. Soon he'd have to deal with that, but not tonight. Tonight was for making memories, not dredging them up.

Chapter Eight

Leah was in her room when she heard the outside door shut. Pressing a hand to her stomach, she listened to the sound of John's boots cross the floor below and wondered if she had finally lost her mind.

"Leah?" he called from the base of the stairs.

Heart in her throat, hands trembling, she walked to the landing. Her bare feet made no sound on the well-worn floorboards. The long whisper of red nylon she'd found in the back of a drawer skimmed over her body and swirled around her ankles when she moved.

Gripping the railing, barely able to breathe, she looked down at John. His hair was damp, as if he'd washed up before putting on the new clothes he'd bought in town.

He must have heard her heart hammering in her chest, because he glanced up sharply. His eyes widened.

"Sweet heaven," he exclaimed, obviously stunned.

Leah knew she'd made a terrible mistake. She'd misread the situation, embarrassing them both. Face hot, she took a step back on legs that shook.

"No, don't go!" he protested, his hand on the banister and one foot poised on the bottom step. "Please, honey, stay where you are. Don't even move. Just let me look at you."

If it hadn't been for his own change of clothes, she would have felt unspeakably foolish. As it was, she just felt brazen, silly and unbearably exposed.

"You look lovely." His voice had changed, deepening, and his gaze was locked on hers.

"Thank you," she whispered, wondering whether he could even hear despite the silence that flowed around them like a dark force. She wished she had turned on some music to fill the huge void.

As if he could read her thoughts, John glanced around the living room. "Do you mind?" he asked, indicating the stereo in the corner.

She tipped her head in assent and he went over to fiddle with the knobs until something unabashedly romantic filled the room. Some of Leah's tension ebbed away.

"The animals are all bedded down," John said,

sounding as matter-of-fact as if they were facing each other across a pasture gate. "May I come up?"

Again, nervousness gripped her with its icy fingers. "I promised you a drink," she exclaimed, false gaiety making her voice rise. "I'll be right down." Before he could answer, she fled to her room and threw on her old plaid bathrobe. She must have been out of her mind to parade in front of him dressed the way she was! Belting her robe snugly at the waist, she hurried down the stairs. When she had nearly reached the bottom, he blocked her descent and extended his hand as though she were a royal princess making her grand entrance. With a courtly bow, he escorted her down the last step. His expression was grave, but his eyes glowed. Slowly, he leaned forward—and sniffed.

"You smell wonderful," he murmured.

Leah could feel his warm breath on her neck above the collar of her robe while his words made pleasure curl inside her. She'd used the scented gel and matching lotion she'd gotten for Christmas. Although it was supposed to be from her mother, she knew that either Rosemary or Irene had picked it out. As soon as she'd smoothed the lotion over her skin, she'd had second thoughts. Now, seeing John's slow smile of appreciation, she was glad she'd bothered.

He leaned even closer, her hand still clasped in his, his gaze on her mouth. Leah lifted her chin and her eyes drifted shut as his lips touched hers. The kiss was as gentle as the brush of a butterfly's wing.

When he broke contact, she nearly moaned with disappointment.

She wanted to be swept off her feet, seduced so thoroughly that she didn't have time for second thoughts. For common sense. Instead John seemed bent on drawing out the wooing of her. Or maybe he didn't even intend—

"How about that drink?" he suggested, stepping back and releasing her hand.

Her eyes flew open. "Sure. Would you like it with Coke? Over ice? I think there's a tray in the freezer, but I don't know if it's fresh. Does ice get stale?" Realizing that she was babbling, she hurried toward the kitchen, bare feet slapping on the wood floor, robe swirling around her legs. What if the bourbon her father kept in a high cupboard had evaporated or spoiled? Did liquor turn bad?

"Just a little water for me," John said right behind her, making her jump. She hadn't heard him follow her into the small kitchen. They'd been working around each other harmoniously in here for days, but now the room was so cramped she was afraid to move. Afraid she'd bump into him.

John ducked around her and retrieved two glasses from the cupboard. "These okay?"

They were jelly glasses with cartoon figures painted on them. That should set the mood. She bobbed her head and stood on tiptoe to reach the bottle from the top shelf. As she took it down, John saw the label and whistled under his breath. "Your father had good taste."

"My father knew his liquor," she said without thinking.

John's brows quirked, but he didn't comment. He ran water in one of the glasses and held up the other with a questioning glance. "How do you take yours?"

She felt stupid. "I don't know. I've never had it before."

"You don't drink at all?" he asked incredulously.

She shrugged. "Well, I did have beer and a little wine in college. Nothing since."

Setting down the glasses, he leaned against the counter and looked down at her. His arms were folded across his wide chest, covered by the new blue plaid shirt.

Heat throbbed in her cheeks. He must be thinking what a silly little country girl she was. When his memory of all the beautiful women he'd been with before came back, he'd laugh at himself—and at her.

"Why now?" he asked quietly.

She glanced away, locking her hands together in front of her and staring down at them. She had an idea that his question referred to more than just the bourbon. "What do you mean?" she hedged.

"Why are you drinking tonight?" he asked. "There must have been other times since he died that you needed something. A little boost, a bit of comfort."

She shrugged. "Who said tonight was about comfort?"

"Then what is it about?" he asked.

Her courage deserted her and she remained stubbornly silent.

"I think you do need courage before you take off that robe," he guessed, running one finger under the lapel before he raised his hand and tapped her nose lightly.

She reared back as though she'd been slapped. "That's not true!" she objected. He was treating her like a child.

"Then perhaps this is a celebration." He ran water in her glass, added a small amount of liquor to both and swirled around their contents before handing one to her. "Cheers," he said, clinking it with his.

Watching him, she tipped the drink to her lips as he did and let it fill her mouth. A shudder went through her, and when she swallowed, the liquor burned all the way down.

"Ugh," she gasped, wiping her mouth with the back of her hand. "It tastes like medicine."

He gave a bark of laughter. "Damned expensive medicine," he tensed, setting down his glass and grabbing her hand. "At least you never reacted that way when I kissed you."

He was smiling, so she smiled back at him. Maybe he didn't think of her as an inexperienced bumpkin after all. Just a woman he found attractive, and not one he pitied.

"Do you want any more of that?" he asked, nodding toward her glass.

She shook her head and he took it from her. Then he slid an arm around her shoulders, holding her in a loose embrace. He was wearing cologne, something clean and woodsy.

She stiffened, suddenly nervous again. She'd only been with one man, her husband, and his opinion of her charms had been less than effusive.

John ran a hand down the lapel of her robe to the knot in her sash while she held her breath.

"Relax, honey, I'm not going to ravish you unless you want me to," he whispered. "Even though you look so pretty I can hardly keep my hands off you." Sliding his hand back up, he let his thumb brush the bare skin in the vee of the neckline.

Her nerve endings snapped to attention and a shiver trembled through her, followed by a rush of warmth that seemed to radiate from her stomach outward. Maybe that was just the bourbon.

"Cold?" he asked, caressing her throat with his fingertips.

She shook her head without looking at him. "Nervous," she admitted.

"Why?" he asked. "You've been married." Then he froze and his hand tightened on her shoulder. "Did he abuse you?" The cold steel in his voice made her stiffen.

"No." She couldn't admit that after the first few times, Gil had apparently lost his enthusiasm. He'd turned to her less and less often, hurrying through to his own selfish end without any regard for her feelings. She'd been too inexperienced, too shy to ask him what was wrong, but she'd always suspected something was lacking. They hadn't been married even two years before he left. Since then she'd been too busy to miss either him or the loving. Until John came along.

His fingers curled into the edge of her robe and her heart stuttered. "You do know I would never hurt you?"

Sometimes Gil had been rough, impatient. She'd heard enough from other women to know that wasn't always the case. Still, John was strong. If he got aroused, lost control—

"Leah?" he asked. "Do you want me to go?"

Her gaze flew to his face. "No!" She hadn't meant to say it quite so emphatically.

He grinned like a pirate who'd just been handed a bag of gold coins. "Okay. Then would you do me one favor?"

"What?" she asked suspiciously.

He glanced down and she followed his gaze to where her fingers gripped his shirt. "Just don't tear it, okay. It's brand-new."

She pulled away as though her fingers had been scalded. Then he grabbed her hand and lifted it to his mouth. Gently, he nibbled her fingers. Sensation shot up her bare arm. Without letting her go, he moved to the middle of the living room and turned to face her.

Before she could ask what he was doing, he held out his arms. Soft, dreamy music poured from the stereo.

"Will you dance with me?" he asked.

"Do you remember how?" she blurted thoughtlessly, and then she nearly cringed, waiting for his reaction.

He cocked his head. "Let's find out."

Leah couldn't remember the last time she'd danced. Her father had taught her the slow stuff and the two-step. Gil hadn't liked to dance, at least not with her.

"I'm rusty," she apologized as John's arms came around her.

He inclined his head. "I'm John." His mouth curved and he winked. "As far as I know," he added dryly.

Leah was still giggling when she realized they'd started to move and she was following him as effortlessly as if they'd been dancing together for years. Not once did his boots crush her bare toes as his thighs brushed hers intimately. Her nipples tingled as her unbound breasts rubbed against his chest. Turning, swirling, he led her unerringly through the steps of the dance.

Finally the music came to an end and the announcer began pitching a headache remedy. Leah stood facing John, slightly out of breath.

"You're good," she said.

"Funny what a person doesn't forget." Crooking a finger beneath her chin, he bestowed another warm, soft kiss on her upturned mouth. This time his tongue touched her lips, seeking entry. When she yielded, his breath caught. His arms tightened. Immediately the kiss heated and changed. Fire licked at Leah and she moaned. He tasted, teased and coaxed her. His mouth melded with hers and the fire burned hotter. He wrenched his lips away to blaze a trail of kisses down her throat and into the V of her bathrobe. His hands slid up her ribs and cupped the undersides of her breasts, squeezing ever so gently.

Leah sank into him, feeling the roughness of his jeans, the sharp press of his buckle, the strength of his passion. Desire swept through her and she reached up to bestow a kiss of her own. His heart thundered beneath her palm, his breath rasped in her ear. She gloried in his reaction to her.

"Sweetheart," he gasped between kisses scattered over her face like petals, "let me stay with you tonight."

The moment of truth had come...the question. Somewhere deep inside, she'd known he would leave the choice up to her. He was that kind of man.

Unable to say the words, she took his hand and led him toward the stairs. With a smile, he followed.

Her bedroom was a surprise, a lot more feminine than he would have pictured, and smaller. Then he realized this must be the room she'd grown up in and not one she'd shared with her husband. It was a girl's retreat with posters on the wall, ruffles around the bedspread and trinkets on the pink-and-white dresser.

At least the bed was a double, he noticed with relief. Not that he'd turn her down if it wasn't, but he'd rather his feet not hang off the end of the mattress.

"I've been meaning to redecorate," she said, glancing around as she bit her lip. "You must think it odd that I use this room now."

Sensing her discomfort, John put a leash on his hunger and drew her into his arms. "Don't apologize. Getting used to the loss of a parent takes time. In a sense, you've lost them both."

"The other bedroom, the one Gil and I—" She swallowed. "I use it for storage."

He felt her drifting away from him. All afternoon and into the evening he'd been watching her, the shy way she looked at him and then away, the soft curve to her mouth when she smiled, the patience she'd shown to her mother. Her grin when she licked salsa from her fingers at dinner, and her unfettered laughter at the movie. So many things about her, the complexity, the gentleness, the quiet strength, attracted him. The way she moved, her scent, her shape, the challenge in her gaze and the way she thrust out her chin—all fired his blood. He'd tasted her and he wanted more. He'd held her and he intended to hold her even closer. He'd felt her softness and he wanted to feel that softness surround him as he sank into her.

"Leah?"

The sound of his voice brought her back from the brink of memories she had no desire to deal with, not tonight. His touch, when he reached for her, reminded her of the way he'd held her downstairs. Her body's reaction was swift and strong. She wanted.

She wasn't sure what to do next, so she loosened the belt to her bathrobe. Watching his eyes darken, she let the robe slide down her arms as if it were made of silk, instead of flannel, and fall to the floor at her feet. Wordlessly, John stood before her, but when she started pulling up her nightgown, he reached out a detaining hand.

"Let me."

Fighting the sudden shyness, she nodded. What would he think when he saw her? Her breasts were too small, her legs too thin. He was so big and strong, so masculine that he made her mouth go dry. When he ran his hands down her bare arms, it was hard to think. When he leaned forward to nibble a trail of damp heat across her shoulder and trace the low neckline of her nightgown, she gasped. Her nipples, already sensitized, peaked and tingled. She swayed.

John took her hands and placed them on his chest. When her gaze flew to his face, he smiled his encouragement. One by one, she freed the snaps on his shirt. Under it, his chest was gloriously bare except for a sprinkling of soft hair. As he tugged the shirttail free, she pressed her palms to his satiny skin.

He was so hot that she nearly snatched them away, but he tipped back his head, his lips drawn into a grimace that was nearly feral, and groaned low in his throat. Daringly, she explored the muscles of his wide chest. Her finger grazed his nipple and he shuddered.

"I'm sorry," she gasped. Before she could yank away the offending hand, he'd covered it with his, guiding her back to the hard male nub. Carefully, she touched it and he sighed, eyes closed. Skimming her hand across his chest, she found the other nipple and rubbed it tentatively. His quickening breath urged her on. Experimenting, she circled the puckered flesh, pinching lightly. His grip tightened on her waist. Watching his face, she opened his shirt wider. He let her go long enough to shrug out of it. For a moment, she admired the width of his shoulders and the strength of his arms. His eyes blazed down at her and a muscle jumped in his cheek.

Daringly, she leaned forward and caressed him with her tongue, like a cat licking cream. He shuddered. Then, with a growl, he scooped her into his arms and crossed the room. Depositing her on the bed, he followed her down before she could move.

Propped up on one elbow, he kissed her, mouth hot and greedy, while he skimmed his free hand up her leg beneath the red nightie. By the time he'd reached her hip, she was melting like candle wax on a hot stove. As he feasted on her mouth, his fingers roamed down her stomach. His touch left a trail of fire. Then, as she opened for him, he lifted his head, took her nipple into his mouth through the thin nylon covering it and touched her intimately at the same time.

Her nerves exploded. Her back arched as sensation overcame her inhibitions. Her fingers dug into his shoulder and she cried out.

"Oh, please," she gasped, mind a blur, need beating at her in waves. Something coiled inside her, tighter and tighter.

John's touch changed, stroking slowly as his voice soothed her, brought her gradually back to earth. When she was relaxed again, lying limply on the bed, he rose and stripped off the rest of his clothes. Then he gently pulled the nightgown over her head. "Easy, honey," he murmured, voice thick and deep. "I'll take care of you."

She was so delightfully responsive when he stretched out beside her that his control nearly splintered. Suspecting that her experience was minimal and that her husband might not have been as considerate as he should have, John was determined to show her everything she'd been missing.

Holding off was a hell of a lot harder than he'd thought, but he managed to delay taking her until her body arched with each stroke of his fingers. Until she pleaded.

Her hands shifted restlessly on the sheets beneath

her. The sweet urgency of her voice shattered what little control he had left. He bent his head, tasting her sweet mouth, and then he covered her body with his. The sense of rightness that settled over him as he claimed her went beyond physical passion, beyond temporary fulfillment. He felt it to the bone, to the heart and into his soul.

She wrapped her legs around his waist, her head thrashing back and forth on the pillow as her fingers bit into his arms. A hard shudder went through John. He gave in to his body's urging and thrust deeply. For a moment, everything in him went still.

When he could stand it no longer, he began to move. She was with him every step of the way. Attuned to her as he was, he felt the tremors when they overtook her. With a joyful shout, he joined her in the completion of their wild ride into oblivion.

A ringing phone dragged Leah back from the most delightful dream. Waking up, taking in the familiar surroundings of her bedroom, she suddenly became aware of a muscular arm anchoring her to the mattress. The phone rang again and reality came flooding back as John shifted, letting her go.

"What is it?" he muttered, sitting up beside her.

Calls in the middle of the night always made her nervous, even though it was probably a wrong number.

"It's the phone in the living room," she replied. "I'll be right back." Turning on the bedside lamp, she grabbed her robe as she slid self-consciously from beneath the covers and hurried to the stairs.

Breathlessly, she shrugged into the robe and picked up the receiver. She'd barely answered when a voice she recognized immediately said, "Honey, I thought you'd want to know that your mother is sick. We've called the doctor. He's on his way and he'll be here shortly."

As Leah's fingers tightened on the receiver, she felt John's hand on her shoulder. She turned. He'd pulled on his jeans, but he was bare-chested and his hair was sticking out in every direction. His face was lined with concern.

"What's wrong?" he asked.

"It's my mother," she whispered with her hand over the receiver. "What's the matter with her?" she asked Irene.

"She's been having some pain in her chest. At first she was just feeling off color, but now it seems to have gotten worse. You don't have to come in to town, but we thought you'd want to know what's going on."

"Of course I'll come, just as quick as I can," Leah replied. "Thanks for calling."

"Is it bad?" John asked when she replaced the receiver.

She explained quickly as he followed her back up the stairs. "I want to talk to Doc Hershaw," she said as she stopped in the bedroom doorway and looked around, trying to focus. What to do first?

"I'll go with you," John said, sitting on the bed to pull on his socks. "Just on the odd chance it's something serious."

She wouldn't have asked him, but relief flooded through her at his offer. The sisters must be really concerned to call out the doctor in the middle of the night. "Thank you," she said quietly. "I appreciate it."

"Get dressed," he urged her as he slipped on his shirt. His expression was compassionate, bearing no trace of his earlier hunger. "And you might want to comb your hair."

All she could think about was her mother as she went through the motions of gathering up some things to put on. She didn't pay much attention to what. When she came out of the bathroom a few minutes later, John was waiting for her. She looked at him and her vision blurred with tears.

Instantly, he hauled her against him, arms circling her protectively.

"It will be okay," he said. "They're probably just being overcautious. You'll see."

She latched onto the platitude like a lifeline as the knot of worry in her stomach eased ever so slightly. No doubt he was right. Better safe than sorry, Irene always said. She and Rosemary would take no chances, and of course Leah preferred it that way.

John studied her for a moment, gave a satisfied grunt and handed her the purse she'd left on the table. "Ready?" he asked.

She grabbed her keys off the hook in the kitchen. ''Thank you—'' she began.

Before she could continue, he curled an arm around her shoulder and gave a squeeze that was almost brotherly except for the way his lips lingered against her cheek. ''No need. Let's get going.''

When he saw that her hands were shaking so badly she could barely get the key in the ignition, he insisted on driving. Of course he didn't have a valid license, at least not with him, but she didn't have the strength to argue. If they got stopped, she'd deal with it then.

The trip to town seemed to take forever. Had it only been hours before that they had come home down the same road? The atmosphere in the truck had been so different then, the air between them charged with expectation. How quickly things could change.

If this was something serious, did Mama even have the will to fight for her life, or would she be happy to join Leah's father without a struggle? Leah felt selfish dwelling for even a moment on herself and what she wanted. It was her mother who was in need of her prayers and good wishes now.

As he drove through the night, John made conversation about inconsequential things, but she barely heard him. All she could do was will the speeding truck to go faster on the deserted road, and when they finally reached the outskirts of Caulder Springs, she had no idea what he'd said to her or if she'd answered him.

The streets of the town were empty, the sidewalks deserted and the buildings dark and silent as she gave him directions. At last, when they turned onto the quiet side street where her mother lived, Leah uncurled her fingers and breathed a sigh of relief.

Then she saw the aid car parked in front of the house behind the doctor's car, its lights still on and its doors gaping.

Chapter Nine

Leah pressed a hand to her mouth, but not in time to block a sob of fright. Please, God, not her mother, too.

John jumped down from the pickup and reached his hand out to her. "Come on," he said. "Let's find out what's going on."

Before they reached the steps, the front door flew open and Doc Hershaw appeared on the porch.

"Leah," he exclaimed, his smile familiar and reassuring, "I'm glad you're here."

Glancing past her at John, he took both her hands in a comforting gesture. "Your mother's had some chest pain," he said quickly. "We've run an EKG and she's stable, but it wasn't conclusive and we're taking her to the hospital in Sterling for more tests."

"I want to see her first," Leah said, struggling to absorb the information he'd given her.

"The paramedics are bringing her out now," he replied.

She felt John's steadying hand on her shoulder and the panic threatening to engulf her lessened slightly.

The doctor looked at him again. "Are you the new man Leah hired?" he asked.

Apparently her life was an open book. Did they know that she'd slept with him, too? she wondered. Quickly she introduced John to the doctor, and then two attendants came through the door with her mother on a gurney. Her eyes were wide with fear.

"I don't want to go," she protested in a fretful voice as she turned her head from side to side. "I feel much better now and I want to stay here with my friends." She tried to look behind her. "Where's Irene? Don't let them take me."

Blinking back tears, Leah clasped her mother's hand. "It's me, Mama," she soothed through the emotions clawing at her throat. "Everything will be okay. You know the doctor. He's taking you to Sterling for some tests, but I'll be right there with you. Everyone wants to make sure you're really all right."

Her mother clung to her, mouth trembling as she stared up at Leah. Finally a little of the fear ebbed from her eyes. "You'll be there?" she echoed.

"I'll drive her," John said as he leaned over the gurney. "We'll meet you at the hospital."

"That's fine," the doctor said, and signaled the attendant. "Let's get her transported. I'll see you in Sterling." With a last reassuring smile at Leah, he hurried out to the dark sedan at the curb.

The attendants loaded the gurney and their equipment into the waiting aid car. One climbed in back and the other got behind the wheel.

Irene and Rosemary had been standing on the porch steps. They both gave Leah a hug and then Irene shook her finger at John.

"Are you going to watch out for her, young man?" she demanded.

"Yes, ma'am. I won't leave her side, I promise."

She gave a satisfied nod. "You call us," she told Leah, "the minute you find out anything."

"Honey, wake up."

Someone was shaking her. Frowning, Leah opened her eyes and stared up at the bright fluorescent lighting overhead. Where had that come from?

Slowly she sat up. She had been curled up on a vinyl-covered love seat. Her neck ached and her mouth tasted of stale coffee. She looked up at John, who was peering anxiously at her, and reality came flooding back. They were in the hallway of the Sterling Medical Center. She couldn't believe she'd actually fallen asleep after Doc Hershaw had left.

"You okay?" John asked. His hair was mussed and he looked tired, but his smile was reassuring.

"I'm all right." She licked her dry lips and then

she noticed a man in a white coat hovering expectantly. He had receding gray hair, a friendly smile and a stethoscope sticking out of his pocket. Leah swallowed and pushed back her tangled hair.

"Mrs. Randall is doing fine," he said after he introduced himself as Dr. Hecht. "Her preliminary blood work looks fine, no indication of a heart attack. We did another EKG and we suspect that she may have a blockage. We'll know more after we get back further results from her blood work, but she's resting comfortably for now."

"When can she go home?" Leah asked.

"Maybe in a day or two. We'll see."

"And if there's a blockage?" Leah persisted.

"If it's a minor one, we may be able to treat it with medication. Let's deal with things one step at a time." His tone was so soothing she could have screamed. "You'd better go home for now and get some rest. You can call in later on. They'll be taking her for another round of tests in a while."

"Can I see her?" Leah asked. There was a big clock on the wall. She and John had been waiting for a couple of hours now. She hadn't slept long, but outside the window the sky was growing light as the endless night finally drew to a close. She felt as though she'd been dragged through the brush at the end of some trail hand's rope.

"Your mother is sleeping," the doctor said, pursing his lips. "But I'm sure a peek won't hurt. Just be careful not to wake her. She needs her rest."

Leah agreed, and he took them down the hall. Before he left, he shook her hand and then John's. "I'll be around later this afternoon if you have any questions when you come back," he said before he excused himself and headed for the nurses' station.

With John's hand firmly in hers, Leah tiptoed into her mother's room. She was tucked into the pristine hospital bed, her eyes shut and her face relaxed. Despite the equipment surrounding her and the IV in her arm, she seemed to be sleeping peacefully. Leah was about to brush her hair off her forehead when she heard a soft gasp from John.

She glanced up, but he merely shook his head and put a finger to his lips. He looked pale and his face was drawn. The poor man had to be exhausted.

He pointed to himself and then the door. Perhaps hospitals made him uncomfortable, although he hadn't complained once while he waited with her.

Leah nodded and turned her attention back to her mother, reassured by the way her chest rose and fell with each breath. Watching her face in the glow from the monitor keeping track of her vital signs, Leah sent up a silent prayer for her swift and complete recovery.

Outside the room, John managed to make it to a chair before his shaking legs collapsed beneath him. When he'd seen Mrs. Randall in that bed, the curtain across his memory had been ripped away without warning, allowing him to picture in painful detail his own mother in a nearly identical situation.

With absolute certainty, he knew she'd been dying at the time. The promise she had extracted from him before she slipped away was as clear now as the taste of the bad coffee he'd had an hour ago, and so was the secret she'd finally revealed right before she closed her eyes for the last time.

In addition, he knew his name. His real name. He'd been half-right, he realized with a bitter smile. His name *was* John.

John Buchanan Burns.

Even while he struggled to accept the idea that he bore the name Leah despised, all the rest of it—everything he had forgotten or shut out, he wasn't sure which—came pouring back, tumbling him over and over like a tsunami, whose rushing water destroyed everything in its path.

With a groan of absolute dismay, John buried his head in his hands and fought down the bile threatening to choke him.

"You must be exhausted," Leah said as the two of them drove back to the ranch. "I can't thank you enough for going with me." An image of them tangled together on her bed rose up in her mind, flooding her cheeks with embarrassment. He had good reason to be tired. Had it been a lifetime ago that she'd lain in his arms? With everything that had happened since, it certainly seemed so.

She'd insisted on driving home, and now, when John didn't reply, she sneaked a glance at him. He was staring straight ahead as thought he hadn't heard her. Ever since she'd come out of her mother's room to find him at the window that looked out on the parking lot, his shoulders hunched and his hands jammed into his pockets, he'd scarcely spoken a word.

"Are you okay?" she asked, concerned for him. While they had waited for news about her mother, he'd been a rock. Now that her condition was stable, Leah longed to discuss what she and John had shared back at the ranch and find out what his feelings about it were.

Had he enjoyed it? Did he regret making love with her? The idea was so painful she had to press her lips together to suppress a moan.

When he finally turned his head, his expression was grim. "I'm fine," he said hoarsely, looking anything but. He looked like hell. His eyes seemed to have sunk into their sockets and the skin across his cheekbones was drawn as tight as the covering on a drum.

What could be wrong? Leah was too exhausted to wrestle with the question. She was running on sheer adrenaline and her day was far from over.

"When we get home, the animals will need to be fed and the horses turned out," she said, mentally ticking items off the list in her head. She had already talked to Rosemary from the hospital. "I'll let Miss

MacPherson know what's going on. I need a shower and a change of clothes. On the way back to the hospital this afternoon, I'll stop by Mama's to pick up a bag for her. Will you hold down the fort in case I get held up in Sterling?''

He seemed to be having trouble concentrating. "Of course I will," he said finally, rubbing a hand over his face. "I'll do whatever you need. You'd better grab a nap, though, or you'll fall asleep over the wheel."

"I'll be fine," she replied, wondering again what was wrong with him. His preoccupation seemed to go way beyond mere exhaustion. Had he decided she came with too much baggage? Was he wishing he'd never gotten involved? Perhaps he was actually thinking about leaving.

Right now she didn't have the courage to ask. If he wanted to bolt, he could darned well wait until this crisis was behind her. Her hands tightened on the wheel. She set her jaw and ignored the ache in her heart. The last thing she had time to deal with today was a disillusioned lover.

Through a haze of shock, John watched the expressions flit across her face. She must be worried, but his ability to comfort her had been swept away like flotsam by his own recent discovery. She hated the Buchanans. How would she react when she found out she'd been bedded by one of them?

First chance he got, John had to call Steve Jenkins back in Seattle, his partner in B and J Construction.

When John left, they'd been waiting for some permits hung up in bureaucratic red tape. John had planned to be gone a couple of weeks or more, so Steve probably wouldn't be too concerned by his silence. Calling Steve was the easy part; telling Leah what he'd remembered and talking to Taylor Buchanan were the tough ones.

When the long day was finally over and Leah was back once again from Sterling, John lay on his bunk in the tack room, his hands behind his head, and stared into the darkness, willing the familiar smells and sounds of the barn to comfort him. He knew she must have expected him to stay with her. When he'd bid her good-night, he'd seen the look on her face before she'd managed to hide it. He didn't kid himself that it was because of his skills as a lover; she was feeling alone and vulnerable. She wanted the comfort of a warm body beside her, comfort he had no right to give until he straightened out this mess that was his life.

Before he could fulfill the promise he'd made to his mother, he had to tell Leah who he was. He didn't want her hearing it from anyone else. However, until her mother was out of the hospital, he couldn't say a damn thing to anyone except his buddy back in Seattle.

And then there was Buchanan to deal with. How would he take the news that he had a half brother he knew nothing about? Would he even listen to John's fantastic story? John had no proof. The birth certifi-

cate he'd brought with him had disappeared along
with his car. God only knew where either of them
was after all this time.

He shifted on the narrow cot as images filled his
head. Remembering was like losing his mother all
over again. The ring he wore was a gift from her—
Mavis Burns. For a moment he longed to return to
the blessed oblivion of amnesia, and then common
sense came flooding back. He was no coward. If he
got through this without losing Leah, he could handle
whatever else life threw at him.

John expected to toss and turn half the night, too
keyed up to sleep, but he'd underestimated the toll
to his body and his mind. His eyes were gritty with
fatigue, his brain a pot of mush and his body an
aching mass, as if he'd taken a physical beating. He
longed to have Leah in his arms—just so he could
hold her—but that would have to wait.

Before he could even begin to figure out how to
tell her his memory had returned, his thought pro-
cesses started shutting down like falling dominoes.
His struggle to remain awake grew more feeble and
he felt as though he were falling, falling through the
darkness into a bottomless void.

It was three days later that Leah's mother was released from the hospital with a nearly clean bill of
health and a prescription for medication she'd be taking for the rest of her life. All things considered, it
could have been much worse.

"Here we are," Leah told her, smiling brightly as they pulled up to the curb and Irene came out of the house to greet them. Her mother fumbled with her seat belt, not even noticing when Leah freed it for her, and pushed open her door.

"Irene, I'm home!" she exclaimed with more animation than Leah had seen in months. "Where's Rosemary?"

"In the kitchen making cookies," Irene replied with a sympathetic smile for Leah.

Her mother rushed up the steps without a backward glance.

"She likes Rosie's chocolate-chip cookies, you know," Irene explained as she waited for Leah to join her on the sidewalk. "It's nothing personal."

Leah handed her the suitcase as the front door slammed shut. "I know." She looked wistfully at the house, reminding herself that she had a lot to be grateful for.

"Would you like to come in?" Irene asked. "Help her get settled?"

Leah refused to be tempted. "She'll be tired, and I have a lot of catching up waiting for me at home." She'd barely slept or eaten in the past few days, except for a few short naps and what she'd grabbed out of the vending machines at the hospital. She'd wanted to spend as much time with her mother as possible. When she had managed to go back home for a few hours, John was hardly ever around. She assumed he was busy doing all the chores she normally shared with him. He'd slept in the barn and she'd missed him, but he was probably trying to be considerate. Their relationship was way too new for her to tell him staying away wasn't necessary. As it was, they'd communicated mostly with notes left on the kitchen counter.

Now she was eager to get home and talk to him about what had happened between them—and to ask where they were going, if anywhere, from here.

"Oh," she remembered before she turned away, "Doc Hershaw will be by tomorrow morning to check on Mama. Her pills are in her bag. She needs to take one first thing every morning."

"We'll see that she does," Irene replied. There wasn't much else that needed to be said. They'd talked every day her mother had been in the hospital. Irene probably knew as much about her health as Leah did.

"Well," she said, hesitating as she glanced up at the empty window, "I'll be calling you later." She swallowed hard, a rush of emotion threatening her composure. "Tell Mama goodbye for me, would you?"

Irene leaned forward and patted Leah's hand. "Of course I will."

Later, when she pulled into the ranch yard, the only one who came out to greet her was Duke. She rubbed his ears absently as she looked around for some sign of John. The excitement she'd felt over being home fizzled as abruptly as it had risen.

She was walking toward the house, Duke sticking close to her side, when she heard a shout from the corral. Turning around with her heart in her mouth, she saw John ride up on Candy.

Whoo-hee, what a picture the man and the horse made! John waved as he pulled up on the other side of the fence and dismounted. Leah ran to the gate, dragging it open and rushing through it without even thinking. Before she could make a fool of herself and fall into his arms, the expression on his face finally registered with her brain and she skidded to a stop.

He looked less than ecstatic to see her. In fact, his face was as somber as a rainy-day funeral.

Self-consciously, Leah let her outstretched arms drop to her sides. Duke had followed her; he nuzzled her hand. At least *someone* had missed her, she thought as John circled around the gray horse and patted his rump.

"Did you get your mother home safely?" he asked Leah. "Is she all settled in?"

She bobbed her head, disappointment preventing her from speaking. The greeting she'd pictured all the way home from Caulder Springs, the joy on his face as he swept her into a passionate embrace and whispered in her ear how much he'd missed her, faded in the face of harsh reality.

John took off his hat and fiddled with the brim, his gaze avoiding hers. She was just about to demand he tell her what was bothering him when he raised his head. A muscle jumped in his cheek.

"This has waited long enough," he said, the frustration in his voice mystifying her. "Dammit, we have to talk."

Her first thought was that he was going to quit. He'd stayed longer than he'd intended. Boffing the boss hadn't been part of the deal, and now he was leaving. Her heart jerked in her chest and she braced herself for the blow.

It didn't come. Instead his expression softened just a little and he reached out to tuck a strand of hair behind her ear. The tender gesture was nearly her undoing.

"I'm sorry, you must be beat," he said. "I didn't mean to sound so gruff. Can we go inside, sit for a minute? There really is something we have to discuss."

Biting the inside of her cheek to keep the tears from coming, Leah croaked, "Sure thing." It didn't even seem strange that he led the way up the porch steps, opening the door and then standing aside as if he were inviting her into his house instead of hers.

Usually the familiar surroundings, unchanged since her parents' time, were a comfort to Leah. Today as she waited impatiently while John went to the fridge and poured them each a glass of iced tea, she noticed instead how shabby the house had become. The curtains were limp, the carpeting worn and the walls in need of a coat of paint. Funny what the mind took in when it was trying hard to avoid something else.

"Leah?" he asked expectantly, holding out a kitchen chair for her.

Heart thumping, she sat down and wrapped both hands around the glass he set in front of her.

"There's something I need to tell you," he said, turning the other chair around and straddling it with his long legs. Even wearing such a grave expression, he was achingly attractive. She remembered how he'd looked in the moonlight through the window when they'd made love. Would she ever glimpse that expression of vulnerability and passion on his face again?

He took a long drink of his iced tea while she watched the muscles of his throat work. Her own mouth was dry, but she doubted she could raise her glass without spilling it.

"This isn't easy," he muttered. "You've been through so much already."

Leah's heart gave a sickening lurch and her stomach plummeted. She blinked back a new onslaught of tears, wanting just to lay her head on the table and weep. Then, with a jolt, pride came to her rescue. It had been a rough few days and she refused to break down in front of him. Her chin went up and she looked him dead in the eye.

"Spit it out," she said calmly. "I've got chores backed up and I need to get to them."

John ducked his head, making circles on the table with his wet glass. It was then Leah realized he was nervous.

"I got my memory back," he blurted, just when she was ready to scream with impatience.

It was the last thing she'd expected to hear.

"Your memory?" she echoed, stunned.

"Uh-huh."

"Everything?" she asked.

He nodded, his eyes haunted.

Dear Lord, what was wrong? A shiver of fear ran through her. Had he been wrong about being married. Had he committed adultery with her? A huge ache bloomed in her chest. Surely under the circumstances he could be excused.

She reached across the table for his hand, but he leaped up like a jackrabbit.

"You can tell me anything, you know," she said, getting to her feet and going around the table to where he stood with his back to her. The feelings she had for him swelled inside her. Please, she thought, let him be free.

"I'll stick by you," she offered rashly. "You're a good man." She was about to tell him that she cared for him when he whirled around, eyes blazing, and grabbed her upper arms.

"You won't say that when I tell you who I am," he cried.

How bad could it be? Was he a wanted man after all? She searched his face, seeing only torment, and an icy chill ran through her. "Who are you?"

"My name is John Burns, but my middle name's Buchanan."

She stared up at him, refusing to accept what she was hearing. "That's impossible. Is this some kind of joke?"

His mouth twisted into the parody of a smile. "No joke. You remember Taylor, don't you, the man you blame for your father's death?"

Frowning, Leah twisted free of his grip. "Of course I remember Taylor," she said impatiently. "What has that to do with you?"

"He's my brother," John said. "That's what my mind was blocking out and that's what I finally remembered." His eyes were full of bitterness. "Tell me, Leah, how does it feel to know that you shared your bed with a Buchanan?"

Chapter Ten

After his confession, John watched the parade of emotions cross Leah's sweet face—confusion, denial and perhaps even repugnance.

"I don't understand," she said finally, sinking back into her chair. "How can you be a Buchanan? Your last name is different. Taylor only has one brother, and that's Donovan. You aren't making any sense."

Although John wanted nothing more than to deny everything he'd told her, take her in his arms and soak up her healing warmth, he sat down across from her instead. She wouldn't let him touch her, now that the truth was out, and he couldn't risk rejection, not from her.

"Actually, Taylor is my half brother," he explained wearily. "I'm sure he knows nothing about his father's affair with my mother, or my existence."

"When did all this come back to you?" Leah cried. "Not before—" Her voice broke and she looked away, cheeks flushed.

Instantly, John caught her meaning. "Before we slept together?" he asked. "No, of course not. I may be a Buchanan by blood, but even I wouldn't stoop to that, knowing how you feel about them. About us."

She had the grace to meet his gaze, her mouth trembling. "It's all such a shock. When *did* you remember?"

"When I saw your mother in that hospital bed," he replied. "Suddenly it was like a veil had been lifted and everything was all just *there,* as if it had never been gone."

Leah's eyes widened. "That was days ago. How could you keep something that important from me for this long?"

"How could I tell you?" he countered. "You had enough to deal with." Staying away when he wanted to be with her, when he thought she needed him had been agonizing, but he'd had no choice. If only he could convince her of that. "I wanted to tell you, but I didn't think it would be fair, not when you were already dealing with your mother's illness."

Damn. He wanted her to put her arms around him and tell him it didn't matter who he was, but he could see from the shadows in her eyes that it did. To Leah, the blood that ran in his veins mattered a great deal.

She sat back in her chair and studied him as though she'd never seen him before. "There's a resemblance," she admitted. "I remember that when I first saw you, I thought you looked familiar. The shape of your face, the cleft in your chin—it's there if a person knows what to look for." She shook her head. "But you said seeing Mama at the hospital made you remember. I'm afraid I don't understand the connection."

"I lost my own mother a few months ago." He cleared his throat. "She had cancer."

Leah's expression softened and she reached over to pat his hand. "I'm sorry."

He turned his palm up, but she pulled away. "How could I have forgotten something like that?" he demanded hoarsely, the pain so fresh it felt like a knife in his heart. "How is that possible?"

Leah bit her lip. "Perhaps you couldn't accept it at the time, so your mind blocked it out," she guessed. "But why have you waited until now to look up the Buchanans? Didn't your mother want you to come?"

"On the contrary, it was her idea," he said grimly. He was still having trouble believing his own mother had been involved in an affair with a married man, even though she had refused to make excuses for herself. As far back as he could remember, it had just been the two of them. "She never told me anything about my father until right before she died."

"You must have known something," Leah argued. "All kids ask questions."

"Not me. From the time I was small I knew the subject was taboo. My mother and I were a team—we didn't need anyone else."

"She never married?" Leah asked.

He shook his head. "She used to say she didn't need anyone but me. The last time she saw my father was the night she told him she was pregnant. He promised to stand by her and to help her financially, even though he had a family. She never saw or heard from him again. Days later he dropped out of sight, and for a long time she thought he'd deserted her. A team of firefighters found his wrecked car in a ravine just a few years ago. He and his wife were probably killed the same night they disappeared."

"I remember hearing about that," Leah exclaimed. "The local newspaper picked up the story and then they ran another piece after the sister, Kirby, was located in Idaho about a year later. After their parents vanished, all three children were put in foster care, but somehow Kirby was adopted and then the records were lost."

"Mom told me everything she knew right before she died," John continued. "And then she made me promise to look them up." He rubbed a hand over his face, remembering how he had argued with her. "What are they going to do with a bastard half brother?'' he asked Leah now. ''Welcome me with open arms? They probably don't have a clue about their father's affair. Finding out after all this time isn't going to be easy for them to accept.'' He remembered the feeling of dread that had made him suspect he might be wanted by the police. No wonder his mind had shut down. What a mess.

He hung his head. ''It was almost like some obscene swap,'' he said hoarsely. ''To find out about my father, I had to lose my mother.'' Damn, but he missed her. He hadn't even been able to get angry with her; he'd been too busy grieving. He supposed it had gotten all twisted up in his head, and instead of dealing with everything, he'd just blocked it out.

''It was a lot to accept all at once,'' Leah told him. ''You must miss your mother terribly. I can understand that.''

No doubt she could after what she'd just been through. Even though his loss seemed brand-new with the return of his memory, at times he felt a year had passed since he'd last seen his mother's face, heard her voice. He could smell her perfume, but her features were already blurring in his mind. He pictured her most clearly from long ago, when she used to tuck him in at night and kiss his cheek.

''I miss her,'' he told Leah, his voice hoarse with emotion.

''I still miss my father,'' she admitted. ''It sounds trite, but time does help. Now that you remember what happened, you may have to start the grieving process all over again.''

She bit her lip and he wished she would tell him she'd be there for him. Her eyes had lost some of their hostility. At least she hadn't ordered him off her land, not yet.

For all intents and purposes, she'd lost two parents, he realized. Her father was gone, but her mother barely knew her. Would that be easier to accept? Would he want his mother to still be alive if her spirit wasn't here?

Hell, yes, he thought. Selfish or not, if that was all of her he could have, he would take it in a heartbeat.

''Where are you from?'' Leah asked, distracting him from his morbid thoughts. ''You didn't grow up around here.''

''Seattle. My partner and I own a company that builds custom homes.'' He thought of Steve Jenkins, his buddy since high school, and the way he'd supported John's decision to come here to Colorado. His mom had treated Steve like a second son.

You have to do this, he'd insisted. You've got family out there and you owe it to yourself to find them. Besides, you promised.

''I thought you must work outdoors,'' Leah commented with a nod of satisfaction. ''You don't look like a man who sits behind a desk.''

''Why not?'' he asked curiously.

It was her turn to shrug. ''You're strong, you're tanned. You move like a physical person.''

"I grew up riding with a neighbor kid who had horses," John said. "I could have been a snowboarder or a golf bum," he teased, "or worked in a traveling carnival."

An answering humor lit her blue eyes. "Or been the drifter I first thought you were."

For a moment they just looked at each other. His arms ached to hold her, but he didn't dare reach out.

"No one missed you?" she asked.

"I didn't know how long I'd be gone. When I finally got hold of Steve, he was starting to worry. He'd expected a call before now."

She glanced at the scar on John's forehead. "So how did you get that?"

He frowned. "On the way here I picked up a hitchhiker outside Denver. Guess he wanted more than just a ride. He took my car and my wallet." He pointed to his forehead. "We disagreed about the wallet."

"Did you call Sheriff Brody?" she asked, glancing at the phone.

"Not yet. My car's gone through some chop shop by now and my credit card's probably been maxed. I'll have to get it all straightened out, but there's no rush at this late date."

Her gaze was on the place mat in front of her as she traced a flower in the print.

"And you were right about not being married?" she asked.

At least that was one area where he could reassure

her. "No, I'm not married. Never was. Lisa was a girlfriend, but we weren't really serious. She broke up with me right after Mom got sick. I guess I wasn't the easiest guy to be around then."

Leah didn't say anything. She just wrapped one hand around her glass and took a long swallow of iced tea.

"So what happens now?" John asked, tension gripping him.

"What do you mean?" She didn't meet his gaze.

Biting back an oath of impatience, he stared longingly at the silky hair that fell forward to screen her expression. "What about you and me?"

"That depends." There was new distance in her voice.

He would have liked to grab her by the wrist and shake her, but he knew that would only make things worse. None of this was her fault, after all. "Depends on what?" he demanded instead.

"On what you're going to do about Taylor, I guess." Now she searched his gaze anxiously. "Can't you just leave him alone? Like you said, what's the point in disillusioning him at this late date?"

"You mean, so you and I can both pretend I'm not who I really am?" he asked.

She didn't say anything, but her expression told him he'd guessed right.

He was tempted, oh, so tempted, to tell her what she wanted to hear, but he'd promised his mother.

"I don't have any choice," he said quietly. "I gave my word. Try to understand."

For a long moment, she studied his face without speaking. "I'll try," she whispered finally.

John pushed back his chair and got to his feet. "That's all I can ask." If he stayed, he might give in to the nearly unbearable temptation to haul her into his arms and kiss her until they both forgot who he was. The only thing stopping him was knowing that later, when they came to their senses, she might not forgive him.

"I've got things to do," he said instead. "You wanted me to check the fence along the south boundary."

She looked relieved. "That's right." She glanced at the clock. "I'd better call Miss MacPherson and bring her up-to-date. I've got some paperwork to catch up on, and then dinner will be ready in a couple of hours."

It all sounded so ordinary, life rolling along as though nothing traumatic had happened. There wasn't anything more for John to say, so he grabbed his hat and left.

Leah went to the window, watching him cross the yard to where his horse was tied. When he'd finally ridden out of sight behind the utility shed, she let the curtain fall back into place and wandered into the living room. How could fate have played such a cruel trick? Of all the families in the world for him to be a part of, why did it have to be *them?*

There was plenty for her to do, bills to pay, laundry to wash, a grocery list to make out. She also had to let her boss know she'd be back to work the next day. Instead, Leah sat down in the old leather recliner that used to be her father's, hugged a pillow her mother had embroidered long ago and closed her eyes.

If he were still alive, how would he feel about her getting involved with a Buchanan? Would he understand that she hadn't known John's true identity until it was too late for her to walk away with her heart intact? Would he care that her happiness was at stake?

Leah looked around the room, remembering how her mother had always wanted to fix it up, but there had never been any extra money for things like that. Even after her father had lost his job with the rodeo, there had been motorcycles and ATVs, trips to Denver with his buddies and evenings spent drinking in town, but no money for a new lamp or a chair or a picture. Now that Leah thought about it, she realized her father hadn't very often put her mother's feelings ahead of his own.

Would he give Leah his blessing and tell her to follow her heart?

No way. He used to say the only good Buchanan had already died or hadn't been born. She doubted he would have made an exception for John—or for her.

She was halfway up the stairs when the phone

rang. As she hurried back down and grabbed the receiver, her first thought was for her mother.

Her hello was slightly breathless, her heart thudding with concern.

"It's Sheriff Brody," said the voice on the other end. "I heard about your mother. How's she doing?"

Briefly, Leah filled him in.

He asked that she pass on his good wishes. "I just heard back on that set of prints I sent in," he continued. "I collected on some favors."

"What did you find out?" Leah asked, a knot forming in her stomach. Was she hoping John had made up the story about being a Buchanan to hide his life of crime? Heaven help her, for the space of a heartbeat she wasn't entirely sure how she felt.

"Whoever your star boarder is, there's nothing on file," the sheriff said. "Near as we can tell, he's not a criminal, he wasn't in the military and he didn't deliver mail."

"Actually, his memory came back quite suddenly," Leah admitted. "We were just talking about it."

"That's great," Brody replied. "Who is he?"

Leah hesitated. John might not want her to say anything just yet. "He's a building contractor from the West Coast named John Burns," she replied. "He picked up a hitchhiker who mugged him and stole his car."

For a moment there was silence on the other end

of the line. "I assume he's going to report this?" Sheriff Brody's voice was dry.

"I think he was planning on coming in tomorrow," Leah guessed. "With my running back and forth to the hospital, he's had his hands full around here."

"I guess I can understand that." Perhaps the sheriff was a little miffed at the wind being taken from his announcement. He *had* gone to a lot of trouble. "Lucky for you he came along when he did."

Leah agreed and then she thanked him profusely for all he had done. After reminding her to tell her mother hello, the sheriff finally rang off.

"Who was that?" John asked from the doorway.

Leah jumped guiltily and spun around, the receiver still clutched in her hand. "I didn't hear you come in." Did she sound as defensive as she felt?

Crossing his arms, John leaned against the doorjamb. "Were you having me investigated?" he asked coolly.

"No, of course not. It was Sheriff Brody's idea to send in your prints and have them checked." She hung up the phone and walked over to where he was standing, hat brim shielding his expression. "You'll be relieved to know you aren't wanted for anything," she said flippantly.

"How'd he get my fingerprints?" John demanded. "Did you give them to him?"

She brushed past him on her way to the kitchen, where she checked the roast in the oven to give herself something to do. "Of course not. He got them off your coffee mug the day we went to his office. Is that what you think of me, that I'd sneak around behind your back? That I'd betray you?"

He straightened and pushed up his hat. His face bore an expression of frustration. "I'm sorry. I don't know what I think anymore. I'm trying to adjust to a whole new identity. Nothing is the way I imagined it was."

Daringly, Leah went over to him and circled her arms around his waist. "I'm the same," she said, laying her head on his chest. She could hear the steady beat of his heart beneath her ear. His hand touched her hair, and then he set her away from him.

"Nothing's the same between us, though, is it?" he asked softly as he searched her face.

When she didn't answer, he sighed, obviously exasperated. She didn't really blame him. "I've got to check that fence," he said. "I only came back to get my gloves. I left them here earlier." Before Leah could think of anything to say, he grabbed them from the kitchen table.

At the door, he turned back around. "Can I borrow your truck tomorrow? There are some errands I need to take care of."

Leah wondered if one of them was talking to Taylor, but she didn't ask. How long was John going to stay in Colorado once he had? She was pretty sure the Buchanans wouldn't want anything to do with him. Then there would be nothing to hold him here.

She refused to think about what she and John had shared. He'd been a different man then, a stranger with no past, a drifter. "Sure, you can borrow the truck," she told him. "If you'll take me to work in the morning, you can use it till I'm through."

Driving to the neighboring ranch the next day was one of the most difficult things John had ever done. "I hope this makes you happy," he said to his mother under his breath as he turned in between the fancy brick pillars marking the entrance to Buchanan's property and drove slowly across the cattle guard.

What would the other man think when he saw the old red Ford coming up his driveway? Would he think Leah'd had a change of heart and was coming to call?

John barely had time to wonder before he spotted the large house sitting on a small rise. It was white, with blue shutters and red brick trim. Down the road that ran past the house he glimpsed more buildings, but he recognized the black Jimmy parked along the circular driveway right in front.

Ignoring his sudden nervousness, John pulled up behind it and stopped. For a few moments, he just sat there, knuckles white on the steering wheel as he tried to plan how best to word his big announcement. How would Buchanan take the news that his father had been unfaithful? Hell, how would any man react to news like that?

Before John was ready, the front door opened and the object of his speculation came out. He was wearing work clothes, a worn denim jacket with a sheepskin collar, faded jeans and a battered black cowboy hat. Apparently he hadn't heard John drive up, because he stopped cold when he saw Leah's truck.

Without giving himself time for second thoughts, John opened the door and got out. Hands on his hips, Taylor watched him approach, his expression slightly puzzled.

"I'm Taylor Buchanan," he said, coming down the steps so the two of them met on the sidewalk. "Is Leah okay?"

It was eerie to see him up close. Leah was right; there was a slight resemblance to the face John looked at in the mirror each morning. Buchanan must have noticed something, too. His eyes widened slightly and then they narrowed in speculation.

"Leah's fine," John said. "She loaned me her pickup to come over here." He hesitated, both hands in his pockets, not sure how to start.

"I find that surprising," Buchanan said in a dry voice. "What can I do for you?" It would be impossible to guess what he was thinking. Perhaps his conscience was giving him twinges for the way he'd gone after Leah's family.

"I'm the guy she hired a while ago," John said. "There's something you and I need to discuss."

Buchanan folded his arms across his chest, feet slightly spread apart. "Is that right?" He sounded skeptical. "Does she know you're here, because if you're planning to speak for her, I'd advise you not to bother."

No doubt she suspected he was coming here, even though she hadn't asked anything before he dropped her off in front of the library and headed for the sheriff's office.

"Why shouldn't I bother?" John asked curiously.

Taylor's smile was devoid of humor. "She's a stubborn woman and fiercely loyal. Once she gets an idea in her head, she's not one to let it go easily. And she wouldn't cotton to someone trying to fight her battles for her."

For all their differences, Buchanan seemed to know her pretty well. John remembered that she used to baby-sit for him and his wife. And look how he'd repaid her.

"Actually, Leah isn't the reason I'm here," he replied. "But if this is a bad time, I can come back later." If need be, could he summon the guts to do this all over again? He had no choice, but he'd just as soon do it now as postpone it.

If Buchanan was curious, he didn't let it show. Instead, his western hospitality came to the fore. "I was going to look at a new stallion my brother just bought," he said, glancing at his watch, "but I guess it can wait for a bit. Come on inside."

At the ornately carved double doors, he glanced back around. "I didn't catch your name."

John had been hoping to explain why he was here

before introducing himself. "It's John," he said, and then reluctantly he added the rest.

The other man tensed as if he sensed a threat. "Is that right?" he finally drawled. He opened one of the doors and stepped aside. "Well, John, somehow I don't guess you're a long-lost cousin dropping by on his way through the area, so I suppose you'd better come on in and tell me whatever it is you've got on your chest."

Chapter Eleven

When John stepped into Taylor Buchanan's house, he had an impression of both elegance and coziness, but he was too nervous to really notice anything specific. Instead he yanked off his hat and clutched it in one hand as he tried to remember how he'd planned to start.

"Come on in and sit down," Taylor suggested with a wary glance as he crossed the tiled entry. John followed him into the living room, forcing himself to calm down. As he did so, his contractor's eye noticed and appreciated the craftsmanship evident in the wood trim of the wide bay window and the carefully matched stones in the soaring fireplace on the far wall.

"Honey, who's here?" called out a feminine voice from the depths of the house. A moment later a pretty blonde who John assumed was Buchanan's wife appeared in the arched doorway.

"I thought you were going over to Donovan's," she said after she smiled at John, her expression relaxed and friendly.

"Something came up," Buchanan replied, and then he made introductions. She studied John curiously as she shook his hand and offered coffee, which both men declined.

"Shall I leave you two alone?" she asked her husband.

John hoped that she would, but Taylor shook his head. "Come and join us," he suggested, reaching out an arm to curl it protectively around her shoulders. The three of them sat down, the Buchanans next to each other on the leather couch and John facing them in a comfortable chair. He wondered how his news would affect Mrs. Buchanan, and part of him regretted what he was about to do.

"What's this about?" Taylor asked. He seemed to be relaxed, but John could sense an intensity about him. He would protect what was his, especially this woman who shared his name.

"I'm not sure how to start," John said truthfully. "What I've come to say isn't easy."

Buchanan's eyes narrowed. "It's always best to start at the beginning."

Ashley Buchanan glanced from one man to the

other with a concerned expression and slipped her hand into her husband's. The show of support distracted John and made him realize how lonely he'd been since his mother's death. He thought of Leah and wondered whether she would ever understand why he was doing this.

Aware of the two people waiting for him to explain his visit, he took a deep breath and nervously cleared his throat. "You and I are half brothers," he said to Taylor. "We share the same father."

The other man released Ashley's hand and shot to his feet. "That's impossible!"

John braced himself for some kind of physical assault, but Taylor remained where he was, absently flexing his fists. His frown was fierce and his eyes blazed with emotion.

Ashley caught at his arm. "Honey, sit back down," she said softly. "Let's hear him out."

John wondered whether she was conciliatory by nature or just curious about his claim. He waited, heart pounding, as Taylor resumed his place on the couch and spread his hands carefully on his bent knees.

"Go on," he commanded in a harsh voice.

Shifting in his chair, John wished the man who'd stolen his car hadn't taken his wallet with the one picture his mother had given him of her and her lover. It might have helped to convince Taylor, or maybe not. His expression wasn't exactly that of a man with an open mind.

"Why have you picked now to contact me?" Taylor demanded, looking John up and down. "You must be in your thirties."

"I was born in Twin Falls the same year your parents disappeared," John replied, "but I just found out who my father was a few months ago."

Taylor's eyes had widened slightly and a muscle flexed in his cheek. "I don't believe you," he said bluntly. "Dad would never have been unfaithful to my mother."

"Believe me, it wasn't easy for me to accept the idea that my mother had been involved with a married man, either." John's face flamed. It was even more difficult to admit out loud. "I have no idea what their reasons were, I just know I'm the living proof it happened."

"Mr. Burns," Ashley said gently, "do you have any *other* proof of what you're telling us, anything to back up your claim?"

John was grateful for her calm intervention. He suspected her husband was about ready to throw him out those fancy double doors. Regretfully, he shook his head. "The only picture of him I had was lost when a hitchhiker stole my car on the way here." He told them about his head injury and the amnesia. "All I can do is to try and answer any questions you might have," he concluded.

"Everything about my parents' accident is a matter of public record," Buchanan growled. "You could have easily researched the facts before you came here.''

"Why would I do that?'' John was growing frustrated. How was he going to convince them? Perhaps he'd been a fool to come here and disrupt their lives, after all.

"Why *did* you come?'' Taylor demanded. "What did you hope to gain from all this?''

"Gain?'' John echoed. Then he caught on to the other man's implication. Taylor thought he was after money or a piece of his ranching empire. All John wanted to do was to fulfill a deathbed promise—and to meet his kin, he realized with a sharp pang. This man frowning so fiercely was *family*. It was John's turn to leap to his feet. "I don't need your money!'' he stated. "I promised my mother I'd look you up, that's all. I swear. Now that I've done that, I'll be out of your life.''

"And what's your mother's stake in this?'' Taylor sneered.

"Nothing. She's dead.''

Ashley gasped. "I'm so sorry. Was it recent?''

Distracted, John found himself warmed by the compassion on her face. "She passed away in February. It was right before she died that she finally told me who my father was.'' He rushed on. "For years she thought he'd abandoned her. She tormented herself wondering if her pregnancy had driven him to take his wife and flee, abandoning his children. She worried about you and your brother and sister.''

Taylor made a sound of disbelief, but he didn't say anything.

"It wasn't until the wreck was discovered that she figured out the truth. Even then she kept it to herself. She raised me alone. Believe me, I'm not wild about any of this, either." He clamped his mouth shut, annoyed with himself for revealing so much. He felt as though he were on trial, but he didn't suppose he could blame them for being skeptical. His story sounded bizarre to his own ears.

"And you don't have a shred of proof that any of this tale you've spun for us is true," Buchanan began. "Why would I—"

"Honey," Ashley interrupted in her quiet way, "just look in the mirror. I think you'll see all the proof you need staring back at you. If that isn't enough, get your brother over here. John resembles him and Kirby even more than he does you."

Kirby. Their sister. John swallowed the sudden lump of emotion in his throat. Ashley's unexpected support stunned him and then he realized she wasn't doing it for him. She was doing it because she saw the same thing that Leah must have.

Taylor looked at his wife and a moment of wordless communication seemed to pass between them. "Why don't you call Donovan?" he suggested to her. "He's with that new stallion he just bought. See if he can run over here."

With a quick glance at John, she left the room, even though a cordless phone rested on a side table.

He expected she wanted privacy so she could warn the other brother of the situation.

The silence between the two men stretched awkwardly. "So why don't you tell me where you're from," Taylor drawled as he casually sat back and stretched his arm along the top of the couch. "And while you're at it, describe the town to me."

John realized it was a test of sorts. He began talking about Twin Falls, where he'd grown up. By the time he started running out of things to say, Ashley appeared in the doorway holding a tray with three steaming coffee mugs, a flowered sugar bowl and matching creamer.

"Donovan will be right over," she said as Taylor leaped to his feet and took the tray from her. "Meanwhile, I thought we could do with something to drink."

Taylor set the tray on the oak-and-brass coffee table while Ashley efficiently dispatched the mugs. As she did, John took a moment to glance around.

The carpeting in the room was a quiet shade of blue. The furniture was expensive but understated, butter-soft chestnut leather, richly finished wood, softly gleaming brass. On one wall was displayed a massive carved plaque of three horses in full gallop. The artist had captured the joy and energy of their wild flight in every graceful line. John could almost smell the sweat, feel their hot breath. On another wall was a trio of colored photographs in handsome gilt frames.

"May I?" he asked after Ashley had handed him his coffee.

She glanced at her husband for permission and then she escorted John to the grouping.

"This is Taylor's and my wedding," she said, indicating the middle picture. It had been taken outdoors with the bride wearing an old-fashioned dress and a wreath of flowers in her hair. Taylor wore western clothes and a wide smile that transformed his somber features. The joy on both their faces was easy to see. John found himself almost bitterly envious of their happiness together.

"This is Donovan, Taylor's brother," Ashley continued, distracting John from his brooding thoughts as she pointed to the image of an attractive blond man and his dark-haired bride. A little girl with hair more golden than the groom's stood in front of them. "That's Bobbie," Ashley said, "and Rose, their daughter."

The little girl looked about five or six. "Were they married before?" John asked.

Ashley merely smiled and shook her head. "No. That's a long story I'll leave for another day."

His hopes soared. Did that mean she assumed he would be invited back?

"No doubt you'll have a lot of catching up to do." She went on to the third and final picture. The woman was fair-haired, like the second brother, but the man at her side had a deeply tanned complexion, almost bronze in tone, and long black hair. "This is

Kirby and her husband, J.D. He's the artist who created the front doors on our house and the fabulous plaque on that wall.''

John glanced back at the horses he'd admired earlier. And he thought of how he'd love to have a few of those doors for some of his own custom homes back in Seattle.

"Your brother-in-law is very gifted," he said. "Thank you for explaining who everyone is."

Ashley nodded, sipping her coffee. "Are you married?" she asked.

He shook his head. "'Fraid not. Do you have children?" he asked to divert her.

Her expression became more guarded. "Twin boys and two girls," she replied. Then she returned to her seat on the couch. Taylor had been watching them silently over the rim of his mug. As John returned to his chair, he wondered what was going through the other man's mind. Before he could come up with anything to say, the sound of a truck pulling up out front broke the tense silence.

"That will be Donnie," Taylor said as he got to his feet. "Your other brother." There was an edge of sarcasm in his voice.

John couldn't really blame him for feeling the way he did. Here came a stranger with a wild story and not one damned thing to back it up. John was lucky to still be in the house drinking excellent coffee instead of peering at the building from outside the fence that surrounded the property.

* * *

"How are you getting home today?" Amy asked Leah, stooping to empty the wastebasket next to the sitting area where Leah was setting out a display of nonfiction books that had just arrived. "I didn't see your truck outside."

Leah stopped what she was doing to study her friend. Amy looked tired today. Her doctor had decided she needed more rest, so she was starting her maternity leave early. Miss MacPherson wasn't happy about it, either.

"John needed the truck," Leah explained. "He's picking me up after work." She longed to confide in someone, but it wasn't her place to reveal his shocking identity.

Before Amy could reply, the phone at the main desk rang. Leah glanced around, but the head librarian was nowhere in sight, and the part-time assistant was on a break. With an apologetic smile at Amy, she hurried over to answer it. While she was talking, several students from the high school came in. They all needed ideas for an American history project and help finding material to use. By the time she was done with them, a line had formed at the checkout desk. When the assistant librarian appeared to lend a hand and Leah finally had a minute to glance up at the wall clock, she realized it was past time for her to leave."

"Your truck still isn't here," Amy said as Leah headed for the employee lounge and her purse. "Was he going to be late?"

Leah frowned and looked out the front window herself, but her old truck was nowhere in sight. Where the devil was he? As usual, she had chores waiting at home, dinner to fix and two loads of laundry to do. Impatiently she retrieved her belongings and then she waited five minutes more before calling the ranch to see if he'd forgotten her.

The phone rang eight times before she replaced the receiver. A headache was forming behind her eyes and dread sank her stomach like a stone. Where could he be? Would he have left town without saying anything? Abandoned her car at home or left it at the airport with a curt note?

No, she couldn't believe that of him, not unless Taylor Buchanan had threatened him. The idea made her furious. If John had been to see him, could Buchanan have used his influence to run John out of town? Would Sheriff Brody have gone along with that?

"Need a ride?" Amy asked, her expression brimming with friendly curiosity. "I'll be done in a few minutes and I'll be glad to run you home. Carter has a dinner meeting, so I'm on my own, anyway. I was just going to grab a burger at the Rooster."

Leah hesitated, biting her lip.

"If he's coming from your place, he'll have to drive right by us," Amy continued: "It's not as though we'd miss him or anything."

Leah glanced at the wall clock. It was now almost twenty minutes since the end of her shift. He had the

number; he could have called to tell her he was running late. If he showed up here and she was already
gone, it would serve him right.

"Thanks," she said decisively. "If you really
don't mind, I'd be happy for the lift."

"Do you remember Carter's brother, Phil?" Amy
asked as they left Caulder Springs behind. "The one
who was working on a ranch near Cheyenne?"

"Sure," Leah replied distractedly, studying each
oncoming car. "I think we were in school at the
same time."

"He called last week. He lost his job and he's
coming home." Amy rolled her eyes. "I think he's
expecting to stay with us until he finds something.
He's got a camper on his truck and I've already
turned the spare room into a nursery, but I've been
treasuring this privacy before the baby comes."

"For your sake, I hope he finds a job right away,"
Leah replied. Vaguely she remembered Phil. No big
intellectual. Athletic, though, and nice.

"Could you hire him?" Amy asked excitedly.
"Just until he finds something else? He'd stay in his
camper and I know he wouldn't expect much in
wages."

Leah stared. "Hire him?" she echoed.

"Sure." Amy warmed to her idea. "I know
you've got that other guy working for you—"

"John," Leah supplied.

"Whatever." She waved her hand expressively.
"Phil could help him. Lord knows you've got

enough work around there to keep two guys busy.'' She looked over at Leah and grinned. ''You'd be a lady of leisure.''

Leah guffawed. ''I don't think so.''

Amy's face fell, and then she brightened again. ''He's taking some time to see the sights on his way home,'' she continued. ''Won't you at least think about it? You've got a little while to decide before he gets here.''

There was no point in refusing. ''Sure,'' Leah agreed, knowing she couldn't afford two ranch hands, even if one of them wasn't getting paid. She'd still have to feed them both.

But what if her worst suspicions were confirmed and John *had* left? Or maybe Buchanan had taken him to the family bosom, so to speak, and offered to let him bunk there. Not that she had a clue as to how long he was planning to stay in Colorado. He had a life in Seattle. Once he left, would she ever see him again?

He was a Buchanan, so why did she care?

Beside her, Amy had started chattering about her favorite subject, the baby. All Leah had to do was to tune in with half an ear and say uh-huh occasionally.

Maybe her friend was right and she should seriously consider hiring Phil, at least if he was willing to work as cheap as Amy thought.

''Is this where you found that guy John?'' Amy asked as she slowed down and turned onto Leah's road.

Leah pointed. "Right over there."

Amy slowed even more, staring at the spot as if she expected him to rise from the weeds and wave. Leah nearly wished he would.

What she really wanted was to see the red pickup parked in the yard, but it was empty.

"I wonder what's happened to your truck," Amy said as she pulled in front of the house. "I kind of hoped to catch a glimpse of this guy."

"Is that why you offered me a ride?" Leah forced herself to tease. "Because of my hired help?"

"I confess," Amy admitted with a laugh as she braked the car. "Even married pregnant ladies who adore their husbands like a change of scenery once in a while. Just don't tell Carter I said that or I'll deny it."

Carter worshipped the ground beneath Amy's feet. Both she and Leah knew it. Reluctantly Leah invited her into the house, trying to remember what shape she'd left the kitchen in that morning. The last thing she felt like was talking, even to Amy, but perhaps the other woman's company would distract her from worrying about John.

"I made a stew in the Crock-Pot this morning," she offered. "I can bake biscuits and throw together a salad." Too bad if there was none left when John finally came rolling in. Perhaps he was eating with his rich relatives, anyway.

"Sorry, hon," Amy replied. "I've got a craving for a bacon burger from the Rooster, and nothing else will do. You don't know how powerful a pregnant woman's cravings can be, but someday you'll find out and then you'll understand.''

Leah's smile felt wobbly around the edges. Would she—or was she destined to remain alone forever? After John, would any man be able to capture her heart? The answer was one she didn't want to face.

''For now I guess I'll have to take your word for it,'' she said as she got out of the car. Immediately Duke came running up to thrust his wet nose in her hand. He shuddered all over, never certain she'd come back again when she was gone.

Leah thanked Amy again for the ride home.

''Just think about giving Phil a job,'' she replied. ''Just for a little while.'' She rolled her eyes. ''When you're married to someone like Carter, three's a crowd.'' Her giggle was followed by a blush on her round cheeks. ''He's such a stud, if you know what I mean.''

Despite her own dark thoughts, Leah had to smile at her friend. ''I've been married,'' she drawled. ''I can figure it out.''

Leah had eaten stew and salad, then headed to the barn to do the evening chores, when she finally heard her truck coming down the driveway. It was growing dark outside as she glanced out the window, determined not to rush out as possessively as a schoolgirl with a crush. Even so, relief washed over her like an

ocean wave, tumbling her emotions until she was totally confused.

How could she feel this way about a Buchanan?
She'd hated them for so long, and now John was one
of them. Instinct told her that was where he'd been
today, being welcomed into a pit of vipers!

It was only a couple minutes later when she heard
John's footsteps on the barn floor. He called her
name. Before she had time to sort through her scrambled feelings and compose herself, his head appeared
over the stall door.

"I'm really sorry," he said, a regretful expression
on his handsome face. "I'm afraid I forgot all about
the time. How did you get home?"

Leah stopped and rested her folded hands on the
handle of the shovel. "Amy brought me." She'd be
hog-tied and dragged behind a runaway horse before
she would admit to the tiniest smidgen of curiosity
about where he'd been. "Have a nice day?" she
asked instead as she tossed a shovelful of manure
into the wheelbarrow.

He was silent for so long that she finally had to
look at him. When she did, his expression was impossible to read.

"You probably figured out where I was," he said
cautiously.

Her heart sank. Somehow she'd hoped—ridiculous
as it was—that he'd forget the whole thing and allow
her to forget who he was.

She ducked her head, examining a seam on her

work glove that was starting to split. "I probably have," she agreed. Finally she could stand it no longer. "How'd it go?" she asked, forcing herself to look him straight in the eye.

Funny, he looked the same as he had when she'd held him in her arms. He hadn't grown horns.

Hands on hips, he looked everywhere but at her. "It went well," he said gruffly. "A little rocky at first, but they seem like nice people."

Leah didn't know how to feel. Should she be happy for him? All she wanted to do was to walk over and lay her head on his chest, feel his arms around her. Tears leaked into her eyes and she blinked them away. Danged if she would humiliate herself in front of him.

"They?" she asked, voice tight.

He blew out a breath. "You and I have to talk," he said, darting a glance at her and then away again. "There's a lot I'd like to tell you, if you want to hear it. There's some you don't know and something I'd like to ask you, too."

"As long as it's not would I go over there to dinner with you," she replied without thinking.

He looked startled, and then he grinned. "Nah, I know how stubborn you can be."

He'd been standing just inside the open stall door. Now he surprised her by circling the nearly full wheelbarrow and gripping her shoulders. "I may be a Buchanan by birth," he said softly, "and maybe I'm just a dull businessman and not the mysterious drifter you thought I was, but I'm still me.'' He dipped his head. ''And I'm still crazy about you,'' he added right before his mouth closed over hers.

He was right, she realized hazily as her senses heated. No matter who he was, his kisses still stirred her deeply, his presence still made her heart soar. The only question—for both of them—was whether that would be enough to overcome everything keeping them apart.

Chapter Twelve

John led Leah outside, stopping her when they reached the front steps of her house. "Let's sit down," he suggested. Once they were settled, he took her hand.

Leah's pulse rate was still tripping along in double time, thanks to the kiss they'd just shared. How could everything be so changed and yet so much the same? She could almost feel her father's disapproval.

How can you let a Buchanan set foot on my property? he'd demand. So many times he'd told her that Taylor Buchanan had been responsible for his downfall, talking out of turn instead of keeping his mouth shut—deliberately going out of his way to get her father fired. No way to treat a neighbor, he'd insisted, his voice sometimes slurring the words.

Guiltily, Leah wondered whether her father was spinning in his grave right now. She pushed away the idea before John cleared his throat nervously.

"They aren't bad people," he began.

Leah snatched her hand back. "You've known them, what, one afternoon?" she demanded. "I told you what they did to my father, to my family. What gives you the right to blow that off, now that you've found out you're all kin?"

"I'm not blowing it off," he denied impatiently, then leaned back on his elbows and sighed. "There's something you should know. Taylor Buchanan has been subsidizing your mother's care."

It took Leah most of a minute to absorb what he'd said, but the words still didn't make any sense. "What did you say?" she finally had to ask.

Around them the air was cooling down, the day ambling to a close as the sky overhead slowly dimmed. Everything was the same as usual, so why did she feel her world had suddenly tilted at some crazy angle?

John turned to look directly at her. "Taylor isn't the monster you think he is," he said. "He told me what happened in that arena with your father."

A nameless fear clawed at Leah's throat and tears filled her eyes. Something bad was coming, she could sense it. She leaped to her feet. "I don't want to discuss Buchanan's lies with you."

John captured her wrist. "Come on, honey, sit

back down," he coaxed. "It's time to deal with this, to face the truth and let it go."

The endearment stopped her in her tracks, even as her sense of loyalty toward her father was pushing her to cover her ears with her hands.

Childish. Like still wanting his approval when he was no longer around to give it. And worrying about his opinion long past the time it should have stopped mattering so much.

She looked into John's eyes, at the steady gaze staring straight back at her, into her soul. Even when she hadn't known who he was, she'd recognized on some basic level that he was the man with the power to break her heart into little bitty pieces that might never mend.

He dredged up a smile of encouragement. Still scared, Leah sat back down.

"First tell me about my mother," she demanded.

He steepled his fingers and studied them as though fascinated. "Taylor never wanted you to find out. He'll be upset with me, but I think you need to know. Apparently when she first got bad, the doctor knew you wouldn't be able to pay for the cost of her care plus the counseling she had back then. The licensed care centers cost the earth, and even for her to stay with Irene and Rosemary was more than the doctor figured you could afford, so he went to Taylor."

Humiliated, Leah curled her hands into fists. "Doc Hershaw had no right—" she began heatedly.

John touched her arm, but she flinched away and he dropped his hand. How dare they!

"Perhaps none of them had the right," John agreed, "but Taylor had approached the doctor when he first heard your mom was having troubles. You wouldn't accept his help in any way, but he still wanted to do something. You would have refused if you'd known, and then what would you have done? You couldn't care for your mother alone."

. "I would have figured out something," she insisted stubbornly. "Anyway, he was only trying to appease his own conscience."

Duke trotted across the yard, his tongue lolling out like a pink ribbon. When he spotted them, he came over to Leah and sniffed her hand. John patted his head absently, but Duke didn't flinch. Leah had always suspected it had been a man who'd abused him and she'd never thought he'd have the courage to trust one again. While she watched, Duke rolled on his back so John could scratch his belly.

"Maybe Taylor was only trying to help a friend," John suggested. "How much do you know about that day in the arena? The day the bull rider was killed."

"It wasn't Daddy's fault," she shot back, just the way she'd defended him so many times before. She wanted to get up again, to run away from the porch and the sound of his voice, but her knees were shaky and they refused to cooperate. "He was too far away. He couldn't get to the rider in time."

John's arm tightened around her shoulders. "He

was drunk,'' he said bluntly. ''His reactions were slow and he was out of position.''

''That's not true!'' She'd heard the accusations, of course, as well as the rumors, but her own father had looked her in the eye, crossed his heart with his finger and told her none of it was true. ''Taylor lied!''

John continued on, like a bulldozer determined to flatten her. ''It wasn't a lie. Taylor saw him drinking earlier. When he heard your father was bullfighting that day, he tried to stop him, but he was too late.''

John ran a hand over his face. ''You know it's true, you know he was a drinking man. Taylor was his friend. He had no reason to lie.''

Now Leah did clap her hands over her ears. This time, when she got to her feet, her knees held.

''I've heard enough,'' she said. ''You may believe Buchanan's tall tales, but that doesn't mean I have to.'' She made a sweeping gesture. ''He wanted the land, that was his only reason for what he said.'' She swallowed hard, ignoring the pain in her chest, the pain her heart was making as it shattered. Tears ran down her cheeks as she faced John.

''I want you off my land,'' she said through clenched teeth. ''And I don't want you to come back.''

Ignoring the stunned expression on his face, uncaring that he didn't even have transportation, she brushed past him up the steps, snapping her fingers for Duke to join her, and went in the house. To her relief, the dog jumped up and followed her. After she locked the front door behind them, she leaned against it, half-afraid John would try to come in after her, and listened for the sound of his boot steps on the porch.

When she didn't hear anything, she finally peeked out the window in time to see him disappearing into the barn. A few minutes later he came back out, carrying his duffel bag. It was still light enough to see his grim expression. Without so much as a glance at the house, he started walking down the narrow road.

It was at that point the deep, tearing sobs began clawing their way up Leah's throat and filling her mouth with the taste of bitterness. Crossing the room, she lay down on the couch and wept for everything she had lost, her father, her innocence and the man she loved.

For the last two days, John had been staying with the Buchanans. The situation was decidedly awkward, but Ashley had gone a long way toward making him feel welcome when he showed up on their doorstep looking for a ride to town. He had spent today on the range with Taylor and now he was cleaning up for dinner with the family. He'd met the children, twin boys and two younger girls. They seemed like good kids.

John guessed Taylor to be a quiet man by nature, but as they rode side by side, he made an effort to talk. Slowly they were filling in blanks, getting to know each other. If Taylor resented the reason for John's existence, he managed not to let it show.

John's biggest worry was Leah and how she was doing without him. Had she hired someone else?

"She doesn't accept help easily," Taylor had said of her. "She was always a nice girl, shy and sweet. We trusted her to watch the kids and they liked her." He shook his head sadly. "Her daddy was my friend, but he was a rodeo bum, liked his booze, came home when he felt like it. After he gave up the bullfighting, I think his drinking got worse. Leah idolized him, used to follow him around after her grandpa died, but he never paid her much mind from the way he talked."

"What about her mother?" John had asked.

"She was a shadow, never stood up to him. Before he died she was always moody and quiet. She kept to herself. After he was killed she just got worse." He shrugged. "Leah needed her, but she shut herself off from everyone, even her own daughter. Leah blamed herself. I can understand why she hangs on to that land so hard. I almost hated to buy that section from her, but she wouldn't take a handout. Without the money she might have lost it all."

Now John glanced in the guest-room mirror and combed his hair. He'd have to go home soon. He'd been away longer than he'd planned and Steve needed him. Before he left, though, he had to see Leah one more time. Despite the way they'd parted company, there was still something he had to ask her.

* * *

Leah was sitting at the reference desk putting overdue notices in envelopes when Amy came by with the carpet sweeper. She was going on maternity leave in a week and Leah would miss her around the library.

"You should see the hunk who just came in the front door," Amy said under her breath. "If I wasn't as big as a house, I'd be over there flirting with him myself." She looked at Leah expectantly. "Why don't you go in my place?"

Leah managed a tired smile. "Nice try, Amy. Don't start fixing me up or I'll send your brother-in-law back to you." She'd hired Phil the day before. His pickup and camper were parked behind the barn and right now he was probably checking heifers in the south pasture.

Amy made a sound of disbelief. "Don't make me laugh. You need Phil more than I need privacy."

Leah was about to reply when she looked up to see John bearing down on her with a determined expression. Instinct told her he wasn't at the library looking for a book, but she did her best to ignore the bubble of excitement that rose inside her.

"Mama mia," Amy muttered, cheeks growing pink. "That's the dude I was talking about. Talk about USA prime."

"It's just your hormones," Leah replied as she rose to meet John. The last thing she wanted was a confrontation in front of an audience, even a close friend like Amy.

"May I help you?" she asked coolly, heading him off before he got to the desk.

Darn, but he sure looked good in dark jeans and a pink-and-white-striped shirt she didn't recognize. In his hand he held a brand-new tan Resistol hat. His gaze swept over her work outfit of straight beige skirt and pale blue tailored blouse and then settled on her face.

"I need to talk to you." He ignored Amy and the scattering of library patrons as if they didn't exist.

Leah lifted her chin. "I'm working."

Irritation flashed in his eyes and was quickly squelched. "I know that, but I don't have a lot of time. Can you take a break or something?"

All she wanted to do was to wrap her arms around him, to feel his warmth and strength, to breathe in his scent and beg him to come back to the ranch. Instead she glanced at the big round wall clock. "I could probably take my break a little early."

His grim expression relaxed slightly. "Thank you."

For the first time, she noticed the knuckles on the hand holding his hat were pale, as if he was hanging on tight. Was seeing each other as stressful for him as it was for her? Then why had he come?

Leah turned to Amy, who had dropped any pretense of sweeping and was watching the two of them with interest instead.

"If anyone asks," Leah told her with a darting

glance in the direction of her boss's office, "I've gone on my break."

Amy bobbed her head as she stared at John with a bemused expression. "Sure thing."

"Let's go outside," Leah suggested, eager to get him out of the library before Amy said anything to embarrass her. "There's a little park across the street." The sun was shining, but there was a cooling breeze. It was the kind of spring day that made Leah long to be outdoors all the time.

John tagged along with her without making any attempt to talk. When they got to the park, she headed for an empty bench in the shade of a huge cottonwood tree. A hedge gave them a relative measure of privacy.

"This okay?" she asked, curious about what he wanted to discuss. Maybe he was here to tell her he was leaving. She had known all along it was coming at some point, but her stomach still tightened with distress at the idea.

He glanced around. "It's fine." They sat down with a foot of space between them. She wanted to ask where he'd spent the last couple of days, and to apologize for ordering him off her ranch the way she had. The last thing he'd probably wanted to do was to hitchhike. She would have liked to tell him she'd done a lot of thinking since he'd gone, but pride and fear kept her silent.

For a few moments, neither of them spoke. Leah listened to the sounds of traffic from the surrounding streets, punctuated by an occasional burst of music through an open car window. From the tree overhead, birds twittered to one another. Water splashed into a nearby fountain, muffling the voices of two girls walking by.

Above all that, Leah could swear she heard her own pulse echoing in her head like a dull drum.

"How have you been?" John finally asked, turning his hat around and around in his hands. "Have you been keeping up with the chores?"

"Yes. I hired someone to help out."

He turned to look at her. "A man?" he demanded. "Someone trustworthy?"

She refused to take offense. "I've known Phil since school. He just got back from Montana and he needed a job." She'd expected John to be irritated that she'd replaced him so quickly. Instead he looked relieved. "Have you been okay?" she asked.

He nodded, but he didn't volunteer where he'd been. Perhaps he'd gotten a room in town.

"I'm heading back to Seattle day after tomorrow," he said, confirming her worst fear. "My business partner has been managing without me for long enough."

It was Leah's turn to nod. She didn't think she could speak, although she'd suspected all along it would end like this.

He surprised her by setting his hat down on the other side of him and turning so he was looking directly at her profile. "I'd like you to go with me," he said bluntly.

Joy soared inside her like an eagle taking flight. For a moment she savored the taste of it. Then her practical side took over. She searched his face with no idea what she hoped to see. Undying love?

"Why?" she asked.

He glanced away, still worrying his hat. "I'd like to show you a little of my world," he replied. "You've never been to the coast and it's pretty there. You could stay as long as you like."

Even before she spoke, John knew she was going to refuse. And who could blame her? He'd wanted to say so much more, but his courage failed him and he'd babbled some half-baked nonsense about a visit as if she could just drop everything and hop on a plane.

"I'm sorry," she told him. "I—" She looked away. "I can't get away. There's my job and the ranch. And Mama, of course."

Who wouldn't know if she was here or not, he wanted to point out but didn't. "You just hired a ranch hand," he said instead. "There's a lot to do in Seattle. We could have some fun." Again, it wasn't exactly what he wanted to tell her, but he wasn't sure just what he was offering. A future together? Marriage?

He was still reeling from his mother's death, from finding out who his father was and meeting the Buchanans.

Leah's face was shadowed with regret as she glanced at her watch and got to her feet. Was she genuinely sorry, or just being polite? "It's time for me to get back." She glanced at the library and bit her lip. That tiny hint of vulnerability did something funny to his heart. "Will I see you again before I leave?" she asked.

He studied her upturned face, memorizing her features. "I'm going to be really busy," he found himself saying, "but I want to thank you for everything you did, taking me in, trusting me." The words sounded so hollow! "You've been terrific." His smile felt like drying plaster. His throat threatened to close up and his chest ached.

She gave him one last wide-eyed stare, made a sound that came out almost like a sob and turned her back. "No problem. Have a good trip." She started to hurry away and something inside him snapped, freeing him from the self-imposed freeze. He caught her arm and pulled her around to face him.

"Oh!" she exclaimed, mouth a perfect circle as she tipped back her head. Were there tears in her eyes? He wasn't sure. He shifted his grip, wrapping her in his arms as he dipped his head.

"Not so fast," he muttered, and then he kissed her. The moment he felt her yield, he poured everything he could into the kiss—his frustration, his fear and his disappointment that she wasn't going with him. Most of all, the love that was still so new and so fragile. He didn't let her go until he felt her start to squirm. Then he lifted his head and stared down at her. Damn, but he was going to miss her.

Her face was flushed, her mouth swollen, and her eyes looked a little glazed.

"Last chance," he said with a crooked smile. "Come with me?"

Her mouth opened and shut a couple of times, but no sound came out. Then the big clock across the street started to chime the hour.

"Oh dear," she exclaimed. "I'm really late. I have to go." She hesitated for a moment. "You could write me if you like."

Before he could ask if that was what she wanted, she turned and hurried away. More confused than ever, he watched until she had crossed the street, climbed the library steps and disappeared inside.

Blinking, he looked around slowly. This was her life—the town, her land, her mother. And his lay hundreds of miles to the west. He hadn't even left yet and already the gulf between them was way too wide to cross. With a sigh he slapped his hat against his thigh and put it back on his head. Once he got home, surrounded by the familiar trappings of *his* life, he could start putting the pieces back in place and move on. In time, Colorado and everyone in it would be just a pleasant memory.

Leah didn't know how she got through the last two hours of work. When she finally parked the truck in her yard and shut off the motor, she allowed her head to drop to the steering wheel and she sat there until she heard Duke's anxious whine through her open window. Phil was around somewhere and the last thing she wanted was to answer any questions, so she got out of the truck, spoke briefly to the dog and went with him to the house.

Phil usually took his meals in his camper, so she ate alone. As she forced herself to chew and swallow, she thought about checking the stock. Instead, to combat the silence filling the house, she turned on the television. Its screen was a blur of color; its sound made no sense.

In a few days or a week or a month, she would regain the relative contentment of her life, she told herself as she prowled restlessly across the living room. Or a year or ten. She stopped to look out the window. The yard was deserted. Nothing moved. There was no sound from the barn or the corral on the other side of it. So far Phil had kept to himself and that suited her fine. She liked her solitude, or at least she had until John came.

Arriving at a sudden decision, she grabbed her hat from the hook by the door, whistled sharply to Duke and went outside. Brooding would drive her mad; the only way to overcome this sudden emptiness was to keep busy.

When she got outside, she saw a dark pickup coming down her road, followed by a trail of dust. Puzzled, she stopped and watched its progress, finally recognizing it as a Buchanan rig. A visit from one of them was the last thing she needed.

Before she could head back to the house for her gun, the door opened and John climbed out.

"Leah, wait!" he called as he hurried toward her, still wearing the same shirt and jeans he'd had on earlier and looking as attractive as he always did.

What more was there to say? Perhaps he'd forgotten something when he left the other day and was here to pick it up. She almost told him to get whatever he'd come for and leave. Resolutely, she stood her ground instead, determined not to let him suspect how much she was going to miss him.

To her surprise, he didn't stop until he was standing close enough for her to see his agitated expression.

"I didn't tell you everything I meant to back in town," he said by way of greeting. "There's something else I wanted to ask." He glanced around and then his gaze returned to her face.

"What is it?" Did he have any idea how it hurt her to see him? Apparently not, or he'd leave her alone to lick her wounds and get on with her life. Obviously he wasn't affected by her nearness, despite the passion of that last kiss. Her nerve endings tingled just thinking about it, and that was the worst thing she needed to be thinking about now.

To her surprise, John grabbed both of her hands in his and his face flushed a dusky red. "Leah," he said in a husky voice, "I love you. Will you marry me?"

They were the words she'd dreamed of hearing, but the timing was all wrong. Struggling for breath, she pulled her hands free.

"Marry you?" she cried. "Just this afternoon you asked me to drop everything and go with you for a visit. Do you have any idea what it is you want?"

He made a gesture with his hand. "I know it sounds crazy, but I think we can make a go of it. Trust me," he pleaded.

"Trust you?" she echoed. "I did trust you. I believed you when you said your name was John Brown. I bought it when you admitted you had no idea who you were, and I understood when you finally told me you'd gotten your memory back days before and were just getting around to telling me."

He moved closer. "I know this has all been confusing for you..." He reached out, but Leah dodged his hand.

"I think you're the one who's confused," she told him. "Do you really expect me to just walk away from my life and go with you, or were you planning on coming back here to live?" When he didn't answer immediately, she went on. "Or perhaps you wanted to have one of those modern marriages where the bride and groom live apart and just get together when both their schedules permit?" she challenged.

"No, of course not. I just haven't ironed out all the details yet."

"*You* haven't ironed them out?" Why was she so angry? Perhaps it was frustration born of the knowledge that she loved this man and she was still going to lose him. She took a deep breath, struggling for calm.

"Are you willing to relocate to Colorado?" she asked softly. Surely a man who built houses for a living could work anywhere?

Slowly, John shook his head. "I can't. It took years to get the business where it is now. And I have a partner. I can't just up and move halfway across the country."

Leah swallowed hard. "And I have a ranch that's been in my family for three generations. I can't just walk away."

"You could sell to Taylor." As soon as the words were out, it was clear he regretted saying them.

"Is that what this is all about?" Leah demanded. "Taylor wants the rest of my land and he sent you here, like a sacrificial lamb, to get me off it any way you can?" Part of her knew she was being vastly unfair, but years of pain and anger were propelling her and she felt powerless to stop.

John looked as though she'd slapped him. "Is that what you think?" His whisper was louder than a gunshot. "Do you really believe I'd ask you to be my wife so my half brother could steal your land?"

Put that way, her accusation sounded ridiculous. Leah's head was starting to pound and she needed to think, but she knew what he asked was impossible.

He had to leave; she had to stay. She was about to try to explain it to him when he took one step backward and then another. His eyes blazed with fury and loathing.

"I was a fool," he said harshly. "I thought you might love me more than you hate my family." He made a sound of disgust. "I can see how wrong I was." He spun around and stalked toward his truck.

Leah opened her mouth to call him back, and then she pressed her lips together. Silently, she watched him get in the truck and drive away without looking back.

Did it matter why he believed she had refused his proposal? The important thing, the only thing, was that she'd said no. In that she'd had no choice.

Chapter Thirteen

The day John left for Seattle, Taylor and Donovan drove him to the Denver airport. They hadn't bonded overnight and their relationship still had some rough spots, but meeting them and staying at Taylor's had been a good experience for John. If not for losing Leah, he might even be able to look back on his visit to Colorado with genuine fondness someday.

When the three of them got to the gate for his flight to Sea-Tac, he couldn't help but search the crowd with the faint hope that she would come to say goodbye. The area was full of people, but Leah wasn't one of them.

"You've been looking over your shoulder as if you expected a tail," Taylor commented. "Anyone we know?"

John shrugged, embarrassed. He'd asked Taylor to keep an eye on her after he went back to Seattle, but he hadn't said why.

"No one else in Colorado cares that I'm leaving," he replied.

The other two men exchanged glances, but neither said anything more, for which John was grateful. Leah had made herself perfectly clear; she claimed to love him, just not enough to take a chance on what they felt for each other.

As the boarding for his flight began, Taylor set down the battered duffel bag he'd insisted on carrying. "It was good to meet you," he said, "despite the circumstances."

"You, too. I'm sorry for the bad news I laid on you." John shook his half brother's outstretched hand.

"The past isn't your fault," Taylor replied. "In a way I wish I could have met your mother. She must have been quite a woman."

"I think you might have liked her. And I wish I'd known our father. Thanks for showing me those pictures of him." They'd been generous with their memories and the few old photos they'd been able to save from their early childhood. Taylor had promised to have reprints made and send them.

John turned to Donovan, wishing he had more time to spend with the two men and their families. Their tales about bull riding and steer roping on the rodeo circuit had made his own life seem dull in comparison. Instinct told him he'd probably never see any of them again, but he'd been away from his business for too long already. Steve had called to tell him the permit for a big project had come through earlier than they'd expected, something that almost never happened, and he needed John back in Seattle as soon as he could get there.

"Stay in touch," he told Donovan. "I'd like to hear from you once in a while. You and your families are the only relatives I have now."

"Take care, bro," the big blond replied as easily as if they'd grown up together. His acceptance had been quick and easy. Taylor was more reserved, but John suspected he was that way about everything.

Before John could stick out his hand, Donovan caught him in a bear hug. Awkwardly John slapped his back, blinking away the sudden moisture in his eyes.

The final boarding announcement for his flight blared over the intercom and Donovan let him go. Donovan's face was flushed, but his smile never wavered. "The kids and the women took a shine to you," he said, voice husky. "You can't be all bad."

Taylor handed John his duffel bag and then he jammed his hands in his jacket pockets. "Safe trip," he said gruffly.

John thanked them both again. Then he turned and walked toward the ramp without looking back. Moments later, when the plane was taxiing down the runway, he stared out the window, wondering what

Leah was doing right now. Had she remembered that he was leaving today? Was she thinking about him? Was there something he'd missed, something else he could have said?

As the plane left the ground and began its ascent, he realized they were questions without answers. Perhaps he'd misjudged her and the situation, read more into it than was really there. He'd never know now. With mixed feelings, he kept his vigil at the window even though he knew he was heading west, away from Caulder Springs. The land far below was bisected by dirt roads and lines of fence he could barely see. As soon as the plane reached the Rockies, he tipped back his chair, pulled his hat down over his eyes and tried to sleep.

Once she knew John was gone, Leah's life returned to its normal routine of work, visiting her mother and chores. Together she and Phil tended the cattle, rode fence and cared for the horses. He was a tireless, enthusiastic worker and she didn't know what she'd do when he moved on. She just dealt with a day at a time.

Leah knew she needed to talk to Taylor about the money he'd been paying toward her mother's care, but she dreaded the confrontation. Whatever his motives had been, she hated the idea of being in his debt either financially or morally. The thanks she was determined to give him would stick in her throat like a bur.

On top of that, she wanted desperately to ask for news about John, but she wouldn't. Hearing about him would make her miss him more than she already did, a bone-deep ache she could only pray would lessen with time and one she refused to lay out for Taylor Buchanan to gloat over.

She'd made the mistake of confiding in Amy that John had proposed before he left. Her friend hadn't bothered to hide her opinion that Leah was crazy for refusing, and she wished now that she'd kept her mouth shut.

"You don't understand," Leah had told her at the time, drawing a disapproving shush from Miss MacPherson.

"Then explain it to me," Amy demanded in a whisper.

How could Leah explain what she didn't understand herself? She'd simply shaken her head, fighting tears, and walked away. After several more attempts to bring the subject up, Amy finally took the hint, but now, perversely, Leah missed having someone to talk with about him.

"Do you remember the man I brought with me the last time I was here?" she asked her mother on her next day off. "Before you got sick?" It had been a long time since Leah had confided in her about anything, but maybe today she would listen.

Mama frowned and shook her head. "I'm perfectly healthy," she said, fussing with the collar of her blouse. "I don't know why you're trying to worry me." She turned her attention back to the front window as Leah swallowed her disappointment. "The flowers are pretty, aren't they?" she asked in a dreamy tone. "I like the pansies the best."

After she left the house, feeling more lonely than she had in a long while, Leah found herself visiting her father's grave at the little cemetery on the other side of town. There was a space for Mama beside him when her time came, and a granite marker with their names and the dates of his birth and death engraved on it. As hard as she tried, Leah couldn't feel his presence in the quiet setting, not the way she could when she was on horseback. She wondered whether he'd finally found peace from the restlessness that always seemed to dog his heels when he'd been alive.

"I'm sorry, Daddy. I don't seem able to please you any more than I ever did," Leah said softly as she left the bouquet of red and white carnations Irene had given her. He'd never cared for the spicy smell of carnations.

Over lunch back at the house, she did her best to banish John's memory and the meals they had shared. When that didn't work, she gave up, trying instead to picture what he might be doing right now.

"I never thought to ask if he had a dog," she said to Duke, who lay in the living room with his head on his paws. Her voice was a hollow echo in the empty house.

Was John still at his office catching up on paperwork, or supervising a building site, or eating lunch just as she was? Seattle was only one time zone away. Did he miss her, or had he already put his experience in Colorado behind him?

A sudden thought occurred to her, destroying what little appetite she'd had, and she shoved aside her plate. What if he wasn't alone? He must know women in Seattle. Had he already cut his losses and moved on while she picked at her food and brooded over him like a lovesick calf?

Leah glanced out the window, searching for an escape from the sudden ache in her chest. Perhaps it was time to visit her neighbor. If she was so determined to be miserable, she might as well be accomplishing something while she was.

"Hey, man, where did you wander off to?" Steve Jenkins demanded, smacking the table with a roll of blueprints. "I've been talking to you about the expansion on the Cameron place, and you haven't heard one word I've said."

John rubbed his eyes and gave his partner an apologetic grin. "Sorry. I was thinking about something else."

Steve's gaze narrowed. "Something—or someone—back in Colorado," he guessed, "and I don't mean your long-lost brothers."

They'd been friends for a long time, and Steve was used to speaking his mind. Although John hadn't said much about Leah except that she'd taken him in when he had amnesia, his friend knew him almost as well as he knew himself. Apparently Steve had been doing a little reading between the lines.

"You're right," John admitted. "There was more going on between Leah and me than I told you."

"I'm listening." Steve sat down in a swivel chair, propped his legs on a box of plumbing fixtures and grinned up at John expectantly. "Start at the top and don't leave anything out," he said, folding his arms across his chest.

When Leah got home from Taylor's, the first thing she did was to saddle Jewel and head out at a full gallop. Phil looked up and waved from one of the corrals, but she didn't slow down. She needed to be alone, to think and to remember.

Taylor told her she needed to face her past—that only then would she be able to move on.

He hadn't sounded surprised when she called to set up a meeting with him. He had offered to come to her, but she wanted to confront him on his own turf. When she got to his house, though, both he and his wife treated her the same as they had when she'd baby-sat their children. Ashley had offered her coffee and pie. Only after Leah refused did Taylor lead her to his office and shut the door.

There he had listened to her accusations quietly, accepted her grudging thanks graciously and, when they finally came, dried her angry tears solicitously. Only when she ran out of words did he respond.

With obvious reluctance he showed her the reports that led to her father's termination by the rodeo. It was then she learned for the first time that he hadn't been fired based solely on Taylor's word, as she'd always been led to believe. Three bull riders had testified to his drinking that day, and the other clown he worked with confirmed that it wasn't the first time he'd gone into the arena less than sober. It was all documented in the official inquiry Taylor gave her to read.

When she was done, Leah set down the report with a hand that trembled. Her insides were churning. "Why didn't you show me this before?"

Taylor shrugged. "You never asked. I hoped you'd eventually let it go without finding all this out." He put the report back in a file and shut the drawer. "What I want to know is why are you asking now?"

She owed him an honest answer. "Because John's a Buchanan and I couldn't handle that."

"I see." Taylor perched on the corner of his desk. "I liked him. He's a good man." Like a laser, Taylor's gaze cut through to her heart. "When we took him to the airport, John kept looking over his shoulder. He didn't board his flight until the last possible minute, and it wasn't because Donnie and I were hanging around." He studied her for a long moment. "Is there a connection here that I'm missing?"

Unable to stay silent for another moment, Leah broke down and told him about John's proposal.

"How could I just up and leave everything behind?" she demanded. "Never mind that he's a Buchanan— and that was another whole set of problems at the time—but you know how important the ranch is to me."

Taylor rose and went to the window. Outside, the view of unbroken grazing land stretched to the horizon. "The good Lord knows how much I love this spread," he said in a husky voice. "I've poured my sweat, my blood and even my tears into every last acre. But I'd give it up in a moment for Ashley or our children." He turned and looked into Leah's face. "Honey, the land can't love you back. Only you can decide which you'd rather have, your ranch without John or him without the land. Sometimes there's no other way to go."

Leah couldn't have spoken then to yell for help if her life had been in danger. Her mind was full to bursting and she needed to sort it all out.

Taylor must have sensed how she felt. "If you're going to put your spread ahead of everything else, just make sure it's what *you* want," he said, tapping her chin lightly, "because there's no one else whose approval you need anymore."

"I'm not doing this for anyone else," she denied.

He lifted his brows. "Aren't you? Think about it." He handed Leah her purse and escorted her back to the spacious entry. Before he opened the door, she found her voice and tried to give him the thanks and the apology she knew he deserved, but he brushed them aside.

"It's just nice being neighbors again," he replied with a slow grin. "Instead of strangers sharing a line of fence."

"You never stopped being a neighbor to me," Leah admitted, remembering all the times he'd offered his help, only to have it tossed back in his face.

He gave her a friendly hug and insisted she let him know if she needed anything. "I promised John I'd look after you," he said.

His words sent fresh pain and regret rushing through her, but she didn't reply.

"When Ashley and I were courting, it took me a long time to figure out what was really important," Taylor said gently. "Luckily she gave me more than one chance to get it right. Take some time to figure out what you really want and what to do about it."

The best place she could think of to do that was the site of her father's fatal accident. Now that she'd followed the dirt track to the spot where he'd overturned his ATV, she dismounted and dropped Jewel's reins. Tongue lolling, Duke flopped down on the grass nearby.

The first thing Leah did was to drag in a deep breath, hands curled into fists, and shout out the anguish she'd been carrying around for what seemed like forever. Jewel raised her head and stared before resuming her grazing. Duke ran over and thrust his nose against Leah's hand, whining softly.

"It's okay, boy," she told him hoarsely as she lay down in the grass and stared up at the fluffy clouds overhead. She was surprised at how much tension she'd purged. Now she was ready to deal with the truth.

Turning John down because he was a Buchanan had been one more futile attempt to win her father's approval, just as her struggle to keep the ranch had been.

The irony was that none of it was going to make a difference. Now that he was dead, she'd never get the approval she'd sought for so long. It was too late.

Once again tears filled her eyes and trickled down her face, but this time they were healing tears. She hadn't been responsible for his drinking, nor was she responsible for her mother's depression. Her parents' problems had been out of her hands and she carried neither the responsibility nor the blame for their choices—only for her own.

Leah lay where she was for a long time. She listened to Duke's breathing and the sounds Jewel made as she grazed. This ranch would never be a shrine, Leah realized. It wouldn't bring him back or make her mother whole—and it sure wasn't going to make up for what was missing in Leah's own life.

Taylor was right. No matter what you poured into it, the land couldn't love you back. But John had loved her—perhaps he still did. It *couldn't* be too late. Love gave you more than one chance and she was about to take hers, even if she had to fly to Seattle to convince John to propose again.

Feeling freer than she had in years, Leah got to her feet and walked over to where Jewel was grazing contentedly. She needed to book a flight to Seattle. If Phil didn't think he could manage alone while she was gone, she'd ask Taylor for help. That was what neighbors were for.

When Leah got back to the yard, Phil's truck was gone, but he had already put the horses in for the night. Duke had taken off on some business of his own, so she led Jewel through the barn doorway.

Phil must have forgotten to turn off the tack-room light. Leah made Jewel comfortable and then, humming to herself, headed down the aisle to the tack room. As she ducked inside to flip off the light, her hand froze and she stared.

A familiar duffel bag sat on the narrow cot. It hadn't been there before. She knew John had taken the bag with him when he left. Heart racing, she turned slowly back around, ears straining.

He was standing in the aisle, dressed in a T-shirt and jeans. His head was bare and he was holding a bouquet of red roses wrapped in green paper. In her whole life, no one had ever brought her roses.

"How did you get here?" she demanded foolishly. "I didn't see a car outside."

"I parked it in the shed. I wanted to surprise you."

Leah's feet felt as though they were nailed to the floor. "Why did you come back?" she asked, hardly daring to hope, despite the flowers. Maybe they were for someone else.

Gaze locked on hers, John closed the distance between them. He held up the roses. "I came back to give you these."

Scarcely able to breathe, Leah took them from him and cradled them in her arms. "Thank you. They're lovely." She could hardly believe he was here. She had missed him so much. "What do you want?" The question came out in a whisper.

"You."

The single word loosened something inside Leah that had been wound too tight for way too long. She set the flowers down with care and hurled herself into his waiting arms. "I missed you!" she cried, holding him tight.

"I didn't know if you'd want to see me. I made so many mistakes," he said, covering her face with kisses. "There has to be some way to work this out. We'll hang on to this ranch, if that's what you want. We can move your mother to Seattle or keep her here, whichever you think is best. I'll cut back on the business. Maybe I can find work here. Hell— we'll figure out something." With a groan, he covered her upturned mouth in a kiss that sent tingles all the way to her toes. She allowed herself a long moment to soak up his heat and strength, and then she broke away.

Keeping his hands on her shoulders, he only let her go so far. "Don't say no. Give us a chance," he begged before she could reply. "Maybe I can't change who I am, but I love you, and I know you love me."

Suppressing a grin, Leah rested her hands on his. "I'm thinking about selling the ranch to your half brother," she announced. Why hadn't she thought of it before?

"Are you sure?" John demanded, looking dazed. He plopped down on a hay bale as if his legs had gotten shaky. "I'd never expect you to give up your heritage."

"It's only land," she replied in a breezy voice, and then she lapsed into giggles as his mouth dropped open.

Leaping up, he swept her into a bone-crushing hug. "You don't have to sell. If you aren't sure—"

"I'm sure," she interrupted. "It's time to move on, and I'm ready. Would we have room for horses where we'll live?" She'd give them up if she had to, but she hated to leave Jewel behind.

"As many horses as you want," he replied, kissing her hair.

She was eager to tell him about her visit to Taylor's, but even more impatient to hear about him. "How long can you stay?" she asked.

"I have orders not to come back until I've persuaded you to marry me," he replied. "How long will that take?"

Sudden shyness made her duck her head. "Ask me and find out."

To Leah's surprise, he went down on one knee in front of her. Eyes glittering with emotion, he took her hand. The other she pressed to her mouth to stop its sudden trembling. ''Leah, will you be my wife, to have and to hold for all the days of our life?'' he asked with a gentle smile.

Brimming over with more happiness than she had ever dared hope for, she leaned closer. ''I'll follow you anywhere,'' she said softly. Cradling his face in her hands, she pressed her mouth to his in a kiss overflowing with promise and joy.

* * * * *

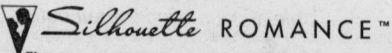

Silhouette ® SPECIAL EDITION ®

presents **THE BRIDAL CIRCLE**, a brand-new miniseries honoring friendship, family and love...

by
Andrea Edwards

They dreamed of marrying and leaving their small town behind—but soon discovered there's no place like home for true love!

IF I ONLY HAD A...HUSBAND (May '99)
Penny Donnelly had tried desperately to forget charming millionaire Brad Corrigan. But her heart had a memory—and a will—of its own. And Penny's heart was set on Brad becoming her husband....

SECRET AGENT GROOM (August '99)
When shy-but-sexy Heather Mahoney bumbles onto secret agent Alex Waterstone's undercover mission, the only way to protect the innocent beauty is to claim her as his lady love. Will Heather carry out her own secret agenda and claim Alex as her groom?

PREGNANT & PRACTICALLY MARRIED
(November '99)
Pregnant Karin Spencer had suddenly lost her memory and *gained* a pretend fiancé. Though their match was make-believe, Jed McCarron was her dream man. Could this bronco-bustin' cowboy give up his rodeo days for family ways?

Available at your favorite retail outlet.

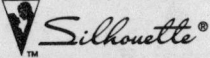

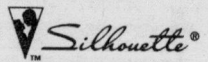